MW00680516

THE VIRGIN
DIARIES

BIANCA ROWENA

THE VIRGIN
DIARIES

This book is a work of fiction. Names, characters and incidents are either the product of the author's imagination or are used fictitiously.

Copyright © 2015 by Bianca Rowena

Cover Photography copyright © 2015 by Tracey Belter, Plumbline Pictures Inc.

All rights reserved.

No part of this publication may be reproduced or transmitted in any form or by any means, electronic or mechanical, including photocopying, recording, or any information storage and retrieval system now known or to be invented without permission in writing from the publisher, except by a reviewer who wishes to quote brief passages in connection with a review written for inclusion in a magazine, newspaper, or broadcast.

The publisher does not have any control over and does not assume any responsibility for author or third-party websites or their content.

Rowena, Bianca
The Virgin Diaries / Bianca Rowena.–1st ed.

Summary: Twenty-nine year old Abby has never had sex and life is passing her by. She's determined to start living her adult life; marriage, a house, kids; but first she must start with the scariest thing of all, losing her virginity. When her boyfriend Ben proves to be the wrong one for her, she leaves on a road trip and falls for Jade, who is considerably younger than her.

978-0-9948513-2-1 (hardcover : alk, paper)
ISBN 978-0-9948513-0-7 (Softcover : alk, paper) / 978-0-9948513-1-4 (e-book)
[1. Romance—Fiction. 2. Drama.] I. Title.

Designed by Manish414 | Printed in Canada | First Edition
10 9 8 7 6 5 4 3 2 1

for my best friend Amanda...

CHAPTER ONE

ABBY FIXED THE COLLAR of her button-up blouse. She was running late for dinner at the country club with her parents and Ben. She hated that restaurant. It was always so busy and crowded.

"I owe you a chocolate bar," Clarissa, her best friend, said. She came into the living room wearing a sexy, strapless black dress and five inch heels.

"Where are you going?" Abby asked, glancing her over.

"On a date," Clarissa sang as she sprayed perfume all over her neck.

"With Mark?"

"No, Samuel."

Abby shook her head. She couldn't keep up with Clarissa's dating life. "What happened to Mark?"

"He was boring."

"Uh huh." Abby looked at Clarissa in the mirror. "Why do you owe me a chocolate bar again?"

"Because I bet you that Ben was gay and now that he's kissed you—"

"It was barely a peck on the lips." Abby's cheeks flushed.

"Did you enjoy it?" Clarissa leaned over her shoulder to apply yet another coat of mascara.

"I didn't *dislike* it I guess."

Clarissa stopped coating her eye lashes for a moment. "It's been over a year of dating and he's never asked you to have sex?"

"He's busy, always working."

"No guy is too busy for that."

"I may have told him I want to wait until marriage," Abby put on her shoes, turning away from Clarissa.

"Are you serious?"

Abby shrugged.

"But is it true? Will you try once you're married?"

Abby walked around, searching for her keys and purse to leave. "You know I can't."

"Abby…" Clarissa followed her. "You can't avoid this forever."

"Yes I can."

"Soon you won't be in your twenties anymore."

"So?"

"So you can't act like you're still a teenager."

Abby found her keys finally and went to the door. "Let's not talk about this anymore."

Clarissa gave her a sympathetic look. "I think with the right guy it will work. I really do. You don't know unless—"

"Of course you think that," Abby said under her breath, "it's easy for you." She opened the door but Clarissa stopped her, grabbing the door before it opened all the way.

"What's that supposed to mean?" she said.

"Nothing," Abby took a deep breath in. "Sorry. That's not what I meant."

"I just don't want to see you sell yourself short. You're just scared and you've waited way too long. I know this great gynecologist—"

"No," Abby shook her head. "No more doctors."

"Your doctor is terrible, he's not a gynecologist. He's just a creep."

"It's not him. It's me. I'm defective."

"You're not. There's nothing wrong with you. The doctor even said so."

"I have to go." Abby stepped out of the apartment, waving bye.

"Tell Ben!" Clarissa called after her. "If he loves you he'll stick around to figure this out."

CHAPTER TWO

ABBY RUSHED OVER to the table where Ben and her mother were having a lively conversation. Her dad was simply listening, nodding when necessary. Ben stopped talking when he saw her approach and smiled.

"Sorry I'm late," she said, sitting down beside him. He was wearing his best suit, the one he only wore when dealing with important buyers. Her mother was also dressed nicely in her favourite peach dress suit with pin stripes.

"Hi daddy." Abby scooted her chair closer to her father. The restaurant was even more busy than usual. The clatter of utensils and conversations floated around, making Abby claustrophobic. She focused her attention on her father. He had grey hair now but still looked young and healthy. She could tell something was up with this dinner, and she'd get it out of him. "So what's going on?" she whispered.

He leaned back in his chair and patted her on the shoulder.

"Sit up straight Abby," her mother said, tilting her head up as though demonstrating how it should be done. "Why are you late? And why are you wearing that?"

"No one mentioned this was a formal dinner," Abby said, scooting back in her chair and arching her back more. She'd worn a simple white blouse with a little lace detail near the collar and a black skirt. "I went to the Pow Wow this afternoon and it was really hot outside, so I had to take a shower first before coming to dinner."

"I don't know why you go to those Pow Wows," Ben said, taking a sip of his wine.

"What's wrong with the Pow Wows?"

Ben avoided her gaze, glancing over at another table where a couple was seated.

"The dances are beautiful—" Abby started to say.

"Ben has a good point dear." Her mom pointed a finger at Abby. "You shouldn't be going out to those types of events alone."

"What do you mean, those *types* of events?" Abby glared at her mother. Her dad placed a gentle hand on her shoulder. She leaned back. There was no point in arguing with her mother.

"Excuse me." A waiter bowed down to talk with Abby, speaking softly. "I'm sorry but I'll need to see some I.D."

"Oh for goodness sake," Abby's mother said, setting her napkin down with some force onto the table. "We've been coming to this place for years."

"Mom, it's fine, seriously." Abby dug through her purse. "They have to I.D. everyone." *Except for you.* Abby bit back a smile and handed her card to the waiter. He was obviously new here and hadn't met her mother yet.

He glanced at the I.D. quickly, then raised his eyebrows. He looked like he was about to say something, but then seemed to change his mind and handed the card back.

"Sorry for the misunderstanding." He nodded then walked away.

"If you'd just *eat* once in a while maybe you'd grow a little and not look so..." Her mother waved a hand in the air, apparently at a loss for words.

"It doesn't matter how much I eat, I won't get any taller mom."

"I think Abby looks great," Ben chimed in.

"Thanks Ben," Abby said, sitting up taller in her seat. It was true that she was only five foot tall and weighed a mere 98 pounds, but that wasn't her fault. In fact it wasn't her parents' either because they were both tall and big boned. She'd always suspected she was adopted, which would explain a lot.

"Well, I suppose the youthful look does run in the family," her mother said, smoothing back her greying hair. Abby kept her comments to herself.

"Yes," Ben smiled. "You both look wonderful."

He seemed in an awfully chipper mood. Maybe it was the wine.

"How's the job hunting going?" Abby's dad asked.

"Fine." Abby took a large bite of the salad in front of her, so she wouldn't have to talk. There were buns and small bowls of salad on the table. Her mom probably already ordered for her.

"Your mother's new office in the city needs a receptionist," Abby's dad said, resting his elbows onto the table and giving her his serious, businessman look.

"I don't want to live in the city," Abby said quietly. "There's too many people and traffic."

"You don't want to live in the city?" Abby's mom chimed in, pursing her lips. "Or you don't want to *work*?"

Abby's stomach clenched. This was why she never ate. Her mother made her lose her appetite every time she was around. "I *do* want to work," Abby said. "Just not with customers and people." Her mother looked skyward but said nothing. She refused to believe that Abby had social anxiety, as though it would be some sort of embarrassment to the family.

Ben laughed, lightening the mood. "Abby won't need to work," he said. All heads turned to him. "My parents are giving me their shares in the business, instead of selling them."

"Oh that's marvelous!" Abby's mom leaned across the table to hug Ben. "This will work out nicely... for all of us."

"Am I missing something here?" Abby asked. She turned to her dad who looked deep in thought. Then she looked at Ben, who had a big smile on his face. He already had shares in her dad's business. If he got his parents' shares that would mean he'd become the majority shareholder.

"Can you even be majority shareholder?" Abby asked him.

Ben leaned back in his chair. "I can, if I get Canadian citizenship."

Abby was about to ask how he was planning to do that, when he cleared his throat loudly.

"As you know," he began, sitting up in his chair, "Abby and I have been dating for over a year now and..." He reached into his suit jacket pocket and pulled out a small box.

Abby's mom gasped dramatically, drawing the attention of diners from the other tables. Ben opened the tiny box to reveal a shiny diamond ring.

"Wait..." Abby pushed her chair back, moving away from Ben. "I... we need to talk." Everyone in the restaurant was looking at them now. Ben reached for her hand and she pulled it away.

"No, I..." She got up from her chair. "I'm sorry. I have to go."

Then she ran out of the restaurant.

CHAPTER THREE

BEN FOLLOWED ABBY DOWN the hall to her apartment door. "Is there some kind of rule book on how to propose?" he yelled.

"Yes, there probably is," Abby yelled back. "Did you even look?" She threw her apartment door open, flooding the living room with light. Clarissa and her latest boyfriend were on the couch, frozen like two deer caught in the headlights, his hand up her shirt and her hair tousled.

Abby groaned, tossing her keys and purse onto the side table near the entrance.

"Just go home, Ben," she said, no longer shouting.

"I don't understand," Ben followed her into the apartment, ignoring the other two on the couch. They got up silently and snuck away to Clarissa's bedroom. "I took you to a fancy restaurant, bought you and your parents a nice dinner—"

"Exactly, you brought my parents there." Abby's voice rose again. "You were proposing in front of my parents!"

"That's what people do, they make an announcement about an engagement in front of the parents," Ben yelled back.

"*After* they propose to the girl first and get a yes, not *before*!" Abby felt a headache coming on.

"I thought you were close to your parents and would want them included in the moment."

"I'm obviously not as close to them as you are."

"Is there something wrong with liking your parents? Isn't that what every girl wants?"

Abby could only shake her head. Ben had no idea what she wanted. He didn't know her at all. Part of that was her fault. She'd always held back, never spending too much time with him in case he'd try and get more intimate. Not that he ever tried. He was always working.

"Okay." Ben reached into his suit pocket and pulled out the ring box. "Your parents aren't here right now so…" He opened the box.

"Ben, don't," Abby said, stopping him before he got down on one knee.

"I thought this was what you wanted," he said, his shoulders slumping.

"It is but…" Abby stopped, not sure how to bring up the real reason she couldn't say yes.

"But what?"

"It's just…" She went to the couch and sat down before continuing. Ben hesitated near the door a moment, then joined her.

Folding her hands neatly on her lap she continued. "I don't know if I can have sex."

Ben's brows furrowed. "Why not?"

Abby shrugged, looking away. She wasn't going to get into details with Ben about how she'd never been able to use a tampon or even get a physical done at the doctor's office, although she'd tried many times. Her doctor wanted to put her on antidepressants to help calm her overactive nerves so that he'd have more success doing the physical exam. She never went back to see him again.

"I don't understand," Ben said, running his hands through what little hair he had left.

"I just don't know if I can," Abby looked away from him. "I thought you should know."

"Is it a medical condition or something?"

"I don't think so. The doctor says I'm fine but he hasn't given me any solutions." Abby played with her fingers. Why was it so hard to talk about this with Ben? They'd been dating a year already. "I think maybe it's more psychological. I mean I've tried but—"

"You've tried to have sex?" Ben asked.

"No, not that."

"Then how do you know you can't?"

It was the same thing that Clarissa always said. Anger rose up suddenly inside of her. *I don't want to try and you can't make me!* She blinked, surprised at the resentment she felt.

"Listen, it doesn't matter," she said to Ben. "I just wanted you to know that if we got married... I can't guarantee anything. I thought you should know before

15

you decided to ask me to marry you." Abby cringed at her words. It sounded so stupid. But Ben had to know.

If she didn't have this 'problem' she would have seriously considered marrying him. Then she could finally move on to the next stage of her life. Everyone from high school and University were now married, except for her. She was years behind everyone her age and it wasn't because she looked young, it was because she was scared. But she didn't want to still be dating into her thirties or end up an old maid.

"So you're one hundred percent sure that it will never happen between us?" Ben asked.

"I'm not one hundred percent sure, but at this point I'd say I'm quite sure."

Ben stood up. "I should get back to work," he said.

"It's after nine."

"You know how it is. There's a meeting with the shareholders tomorrow and I have to be ready."

"Okay." Abby got up too. A lump was forming in her throat, making it hard to speak. "Should we talk about this tomorrow, or...?"

"I've got a lot on my plate, with all the changes going on in the company." Ben walked to the door and Abby followed him. "Actually I'm going away on business for a few weeks."

"But what about my parents' anniversary party, you said—"

"I'll see you around Abby," Ben opened the door and left, without looking back.

Abby clenched her fists tight, holding back the tears that threatened to flow. She was hopeless. No man would love her if she didn't have sex with them. Unable to hold back the sobs any longer, she ran to her room and slammed the door shut.

CHAPTER FOUR

ABBY TRIED NOT TO SLAM the door as she got into the driver's seat of her mom's company minivan. Clarissa was already asleep in the passenger seat. She was always up for an adventure, even when she was half asleep.

Abby rolled down the window to let the sweet scents of the morning in. It was 5 a.m. and they were leaving town, their destination yet to be decided. The roads were empty and the perfectly mowed neighbourhood was quiet. Ahead the sunrise grew brighter. There was hope and excitement in its orange and yellow rays, a promise of new possibilities. Abby's hand shook as she started the ignition and put the van into drive.

"Quit thinking so hard, you're giving me a headache," Clarissa said, her eyes now open.

"Sorry." Abby smiled at her. "I thought you were asleep. How are you feeling? I know early mornings aren't your thing."

Clarissa shrugged. "You're finally rebelling. I couldn't say no to that, or have you chicken out! No way. I have to see this happen first hand."

"I'm not rebelling," Abby said. She glanced into the rear view mirror, then side mirrors, then back at the rear view mirror again.

"Are you worried your parents sent the cops after you?"

"Hopefully they won't even notice I'm gone, for a little while at least. They're going on their 35th anniversary cruise." Abby sighed heavily. "I don't know what I'm doing anymore, Clarissa."

"We don't have to leave town," Clarissa said with gentleness in her voice. "We could just pig out on lactose-free ice cream and watch vampire movies all day instead."

"No, I need to do this." Abby frowned, concentrating on the road far more than necessary. Tears stung at her eyes. She likely had the worst case of separation anxiety known to any adult. But that was exactly why she had to do this, to separate herself from her parents. She never went on trips without them. She didn't go out to the bar, take weekend trips to Vegas or rebelled in any way, because she was too scared. Scared of getting hurt, scared of life, scared of love and *especially* terrified of having sex.

In a few weeks she'd be turning thirty. THIRTY! She pushed down on the gas pedal. Forget Ben and her parents. She was leaving town and never looking back.

"Where are we going anyway? You never told me," Clarissa asked.

"We're going to chase after the sun until we catch it."

"Always the poet," Clarissa laughed. "Sounds good to me." She pulled off her jacket and set it over her face to block out the sun which was now coming over the horizon. "Well then I hope you brought your sunglasses."

CHAPTER FIVE

BRIGHT STUDIO LIGHTS WARMED Abby's face and shoulders like the sun as she looked out into the audience. She tried to see the people but they were just a dark sea of heads. She'd had dreams like this before; public speaking while naked or trapped in a crowd, but she'd never had one about a talk show before.

"Welcome back to the show!" Adam Whyte, the host of Abby's favourite talk show, smiled into the cameras. He looked less attractive close up, his stage makeup noticeable at the neckline. Abby could smell his cologne from where she was seated opposite him, their chairs turned at an angle to face the audience.

"Today we have Abby Blosym with us. She is a twenty-nine year old virgin!"

The crowd erupted in shouts of disbelief and laughter. Abby's stomach plummeted. She looked for an escape but was stuck to her chair, trapped in a nightmare that felt all too real. Knowing it was just a dream didn't seem to help as she looked out at the audience.

"Tell us Abby," Adam Whyte continued, his fake smile frightening. "How long have you and Ben been married?"

"Two years," Abby said, her quiet voice amplified by the microphone on her lapel. She looked down, surprised to see that she wearing one of her mother's dress suits, the peach coloured one with grey pin stripes. It fit big and the top was too open, showing more of her chest than she was comfortable with. She grasped the front with both her hands, pulling the suit jacket together.

"Two whole years…" Adam's brows furrowed in an overacted display of concern. "Tell us Abby, why this loveless marriage?"

"My marriage isn't loveless…"

"Do you like men?"

"Yes, of course!" Angry tears stung at Abby's eyes. She wanted to defend herself, but didn't know how.

"It looks like we have a question from the audience."

An assistant took a microphone to a large man in the crowd who was wearing a construction worker's vest and white tank top.

"If you come home with me sweetheart you won't be a virgin anymore," he said, his grin showcasing missing teeth in the front.

Hoots and hollers from the audience deepened the heat in Abby's cheeks. Before she could reply, the assistant handed the mic to another audience member.

"Have you seen your doctor?" an elderly lady asked.

"There won't be a need for that!" Adam announced, his hands motioning excitedly. "We've got world renowned gynecologist Larry Browne with us today! He will be doing an examination on Abby right here on the show!"

Abby woke with a start, heart pounding and body dripping with sweat. Her head still resonated with the sounds of the audience hollering and cheering at her expense. She sat up and wiped her tears with the back of her hand.

The dark room gave no clue as to her where she was. According to the digital clock by the bed it was 11:45 PM. They'd arrived here around supper time, then basically collapsed onto the beds as soon as they got into the hotel room. Abby had driven for over eight hours, something she'd never done before in her life.

A sound, like the lapping of waves, drifted in from the open window. Along with it, laughter and the chattering of people. Had they reached the ocean? She hadn't been paying attention to the road signs all that much. She was too upset by the text she'd gotten from Ben saying he'd be away on a business trip for a few weeks, his way of avoiding her.

Most of the drive had been a blur of mountains and trees before they finally decided to stop at the next town. Now they were at a beach-like destination but Abby had no idea where.

She got out of bed and walked to the window, then pulled the curtains aside. Cars drove to and fro on a beachfront road, their engine sounds were what had sounded like waves. Down below, groups of tanned tourists made their way leisurely down the sidewalks.

Abby tugged at her t-shirt which was stuck to her damp back. Strands of her long hair had escaped her braid and now clung to her cheek. She pulled the hair away, unaccustomed to such sticky humidity.

The large hotel sign outside the window lit up the room and Abby turned to see Clarissa sprawled out on the sheets, looking as overheated as Abby felt. The poor girl hadn't slept a wink on the long drive today, despite getting no sleep the previous night. She'd come home late from a party, then packed to leave on this impromptu trip.

Abby went to her suitcase and looked for a change of clothes. She pulled out the only summer dress she owned, a light green t-shirt dress. After getting changed, she wrote Clarissa a note then quietly left the hotel room.

A gentle breeze of fresh air greeted her when she stepped outside. In it was the scent of newly cut grass after a recent rain. There was also the smell of lake water, coconut sunblock lotion and a smoky barbeque from a nearby restaurant.

The air was thick with moisture and Abby smiled. She'd lived her entire life in the prairies where the air was dry and smelled like cattle manure. This was like paradise.

Across the street, dark waters stretched out vast and motionless. Abby remembered lively waves earlier that day when they'd driven down the beachfront road, all the motor boat activity causing waves to lap the shore. Now the waters were still, as though resting for the night.

Fake palm trees lit up in red, green and yellow drew attention to a nearby pub with a pirate's theme. There was a crowd waiting outside its front entrance where a podium was set up for taking reservations. Abby headed in the opposite direction to the nearest cross-walk, anxious to get to the other side where it was less crowded.

She stood straighter as she walked, throwing her shoulders back and gathering her courage. It had to be about midnight now. Her mother would have a heart attack if she knew that her daughter was out walking the streets at midnight.

Needing to prove to herself that she no longer had to worry about her mom's opinions on her life and actions, Abby jumped down from the sidewalk onto the cool sand. The beach stretched out before it reached the water's edge. She took off her sandals and walked towards the water.

When her toes touched the water Abby let out a small giggle. This place was magical, and she'd discovered it all on her own. No one back home knew where she was. She was free. For now.

CHAPTER SIX

THE SOUND OF LAUGHTER bounced off the smooth surface of the water. Abby could see the floating dock in the distance by the light of the full moon. Rowdy teenagers, or maybe college kids, were jumping into the water. What would it have been like to grow up in a place like this, coming to the beach every day in the summer?

The water looked black and menacing beneath the night sky. Abby reached down and dipped her fingers into it. It felt warm to her hands, but cold to her feet. Its black luster was simply an illusion; she could see her hand through the water which was clear.

"Are you coming in?"

Abby jumped up. "Who's there?" she said, looking around.

A young guy, probably from the group out on the dock, approached from the water. He shook his wet hair, the drops reaching the bare skin on Abby's arms. "The Ogopogo," he said.

"The what?"

He came closer. "The monster that lives in this lake."

"A monster lives in this lake?" Abby backed away.

He laughed and she turned to leave. She wasn't going to talk with a stranger, no matter how attractive he was. He could drown her in the lake and no one would hear her screams. Abby sighed, disappointed. So this was a lake and she hadn't reached the Ocean after all.

"Wait." The boy rushed out of the water and caught up to her. "I'm not making fun of you or anything, I promise."

Abby stopped and turned to face him. She liked the sound of his voice and was curious to get a closer look at him.

"There really is a legend of a lake monster," he continued. Now that he was closer she could see his blue eyes, which glistened in the light of the street lamp. He stood only slightly taller than her and had a slim build with firm muscles. "Or a dinosaur of some sort maybe, or a large snake, no one's sure exactly what it is. It's called the Ogopogo." He smiled. "All the gift shops have Ogopogo t-shirts and stuffed animals. How long have you been here?"

"I haven't been in a gift shop yet," Abby said, her body tensing under his gaze.

"What brings you to Penticton?" he asked, running a hand through his thick wavy hair to move it out of his eyes.

"I was…headed for the ocean."

"Oh." His smile brightened. "My name's Jade."

Abby nodded but didn't offer her name, unable to shut out her mother's warning voice playing in her head. *Stranger danger.*

"You're not far from the ocean," he said. "Another five or six hours west and you'd be there."

"Well, then we almost made it." Abby looked out over the waters again. To her right the lights of the beachside establishments along the shore reflected in the water as far as the eye could see. To her left the lake seemed to end at an old fashion cruise ship, covered in thousands of tiny lights. "The ocean couldn't be more beautiful than this anyway," she said.

"It isn't," Jade said. "At least not to me. This is my favourite place in the world."

Abby smiled. The ship's festive lighting made it seem like there was a party going on inside at that very moment. She wanted to be in there, dressed in a fancy 19th century gown and eating delicacies. "It's beautiful," she whispered.

"That's the S.S. Sicamous," Jade said.

Abby headed to the water again. This time she didn't stop at the water's edge, but waded in. It felt warm to her feet, which had gotten wet previously, and cold to the rest of her. She heard splashes behind her as Jade followed in after her. When the hem of her summer dress touched the top of the water Abby stopped.

That's far enough, her mother's voice filled her thoughts. A memory long forgotten, now resurfaced. They'd taken a trip to a cabin at a lake, long ago when she was in grade one. *You'll get your dress wet. Stop acting childish. Grow up.*

Closing her eyes Abby let herself fall forward into the lake. A small gasp escaped her at the sudden shock of cold. Jade was already in the water beside her.

"I like to pretend I fell overboard," he nodded towards the S.S. Sicamous.

"Or, more likely, were forced to walk the plank," Abby teased. Her tummy did a little flip when she realized how close Jade was to her in the water. She never joked around with guys, but with him it seemed easy. Maybe because he was younger than the men she'd been dating in the last five years. Before then, she hadn't dated at all, not in high school or even college. She'd been too focused on her studies, and for what? Her two degrees basically made her over qualified and undesired by employers, unless she moved to a big city like Toronto and got a high stress job.

"Yes," Jade said, coming in even closer.

"Yes what?" Abby blinked.

"I was forced to walk the plank," he continued with a mischievous look in his eyes. "Thrown overboard by pirates, by my own crew actually. I was their captain."

Abby evaded him and swam ahead, her tummy flips increasing by the second.

"Does the Sicamous ever get taken out onto the water?" she asked as she swam. Now that her body was used to the lake temperature it didn't feel cold anymore but somewhat pleasant.

"No, it's a museum now, permanently docked."

"Oh that's so cool!" Abby said. "I want to go. Is it open right now?"

"It's past midnight. This isn't exactly Vegas." Jade winked at her and she swam faster, trying to put a little distance between them.

"All the lights are on, so, I just thought maybe it was open," she said over her shoulder.

No matter how far they went, they never seemed to be getting any closer to the ship. Abby stopped to check if her feet could still touch the bottom. Her toes sunk into the soft sand and she breathed a sigh of relief. Jade moved in close beside her.

"I was thinking of going to check it out tomorrow," he said.

Abby swam ahead of him. Suddenly her feet touched something slimy and she screamed, kicking at it to get it off. She'd gotten tangled in weeds. The thought of the long underwater grass extending up from deep within the dark waters made her shiver. The more she kicked the more the weeds tangled her legs. All she could muster was a strangled cry.

"You okay?" Jade reached down into the water and pulled the weeds off her legs. The lake floor was suddenly much deeper here and Abby couldn't reach. Jade grabbed her around the waist and pulled her back to the shallower water where there was sand and no weeds. His fingers had a good grasp on her hips and the heat from his hands seeped through her thin dress, spreading over her body.

Abby reached her toes down and they touched the sand. She was safe. With a shove she pushed Jade away from her. "Don't touch me!"

Jade lifted his hands out of the water and put them up in surrender. "Sorry."

"I..." She looked all around for a quick escape but was surrounded by a sea of black water. Jade had a worried expression on his face as he watched her. She turned away. It wasn't the scary weeds that made her heart pound at the moment, but the feel of Jade's hands on her waist as he'd pulled her out.

"There's probably more weeds that way," Jade said, pointing towards the S.S. Sicamous. He'd dropped his flirtatious manner and now seemed subdued, probably because she'd yelled at him when he was only trying to help.

"I have to go," Abby said, heading for the shore. Her mind was suddenly overrun by illogical fears of sea creatures and dark whirlpools. Jade called after her but she kept swimming even faster. This time he wasn't able to catch up. The adrenaline drove her forward. She had to get back to the hotel, away from the black lake and the dinosaur-sized monster that lived in it, and away from the boy who made her heat up with just one simple touch.

CHAPTER SEVEN

"COME ON ABBY, we've been here for hours!" Clarissa whined.

They'd been wandering the historic S.S. Sicamous ship all morning and had even gone up to the very top to look out over the lake. Coming to the museum was the only thing Abby could think of to do to find Jade, since he mentioned going to see it today. She wanted to see him again and to apologize for the way she'd overreacted.

There was no sign of him anywhere.

If only she hadn't freaked out and run away. Maybe this was for the best. He was too young for her anyway.

The museum had a relaxed atmosphere, with all the vacationers mulling about. It felt good to be away from home and her parents, and from Ben.

"Let's go," Clarissa said, pulling on Abby's arm.

A group of children had gathered around the scale model of the Kettle Valley Railway. The little train ran along the winding tracks through the Kettle Valley, past the tiny towns with historic buildings and through tunnels in the small mountain.

Abby smiled, watching the kids follow the small train around in excitement. The idea that she had the ability to produce one of these lively little human beings was so amazing. But at the rate she was going in life she'd run out of time before she ever had one of her own.

Clarissa tugged at Abby's sleeve again. "Come on..."

"I just have one more question for the tour guide," Abby said.

"No more questions for the tour guide. Let's go to that carnival place!" Clarissa dragged Abby out of the S.S. Sicamous and into the sun. "I want to go there." She pointed to a theme park in the distance, with a large boat at the center.

Abby lifted her hand to block out the sun. "Looks loud and rowdy. We could just sit by the water—"

"So you can watch the museum doors?" Clarissa crossed her arms.

Abby shrugged. "No, but—"

"Did your horoscope say you'd be meeting a tall, dark and handsome stranger at a museum today or something?"

"No."

"Do you have the hots for the tour guide?"

"No!" Abby laughed.

"Then come on! I'm starving. There's got to be some food over there." Clarissa linked arms with Abby and they headed for the amusement park.

* * *

The sign above the entrance read ADVENTURE PARK as Abby and Clarissa walked in. To the right, was a wooden pirate's ship about the size of Abby's minivan. It had cast-iron cannons and everything. A pond ran all the way around the concession area, where the tickets were sold for the rides. Clarissa got in line, silent as she looked around.

Abby searched the crowd for a head of dark, wavy hair. This was a popular place, maybe Jade was here somewhere.

"They've got hot dogs…" Clarissa said, looking at the menu above. Abby clung to her friend's arm as more people joined the lineup, crowding around close.

"I don't eat hot dogs," she said, breathing deeply to control her heart rate. *It's just like the country club on a busy day, no big deal.*

"Ice cream?" Clarissa asked.

"What? Oh, no thanks. You know I can't have ice cream."

"Nachos!" Clarissa clapped her hands together. "Yum!"

"I can't have the cheese."

"You have to eat something."

It was their turn to order.

After getting food for herself, Clarissa found a shaded area while Abby checked out the pond. Its dark waters reminded her of the lake at night. Now, in the heat of the day, meeting Jade seemed like only a dream. Maybe she had dreamed it.

The sun beat down from above, making Abby long to be in the cool water again, preferably with Jade. He seemed permanently imbedded in her mind, even though she'd just met him once. There was something addicting about his easy going manner and charm. She admired that. And there was something else, an attraction that she couldn't explain.

There had to be someone who'd seen him around. He was quite an attractive guy and would have turned a few heads. It was a longshot but Abby headed to the concession counter again. There was no longer a line up now that the crowd from earlier had passed through.

"I have a silly question for you," Abby said to the lively girl at the front counter.

"Yes?" she smiled. Her pony tail bobbed about as she kept busy.

"You wouldn't happen to have seen a young guy, about nineteen or twenty, maybe older, with dark wavy hair and blue eyes would you?" Abby asked, fidgeting with her braid.

The girl thought about this for a moment. "How long ago was he here?"

"I'm not sure if he was here, exactly. I was just wondering..."

"What was he wearing?"

Abby blushed. Jade had been shirtless and wearing swim trunks when she'd last seen him. "I'm not sure."

"There's a church youth conference thing going on at the other beach," the concession girl said. "My cousin is there. Lots of cute guys over there I've heard."

Abby raised her eyebrows. "There's another beach?"

"Yes. On the other side of town. Lake Skaha."

"Okay. Thanks."

Abby ran to get Clarissa, who was still eating at a table in the shade.

"We're going to Lake Skaha!" Abby said, grabbing her arm.

"Where?" Clarissa asked. She shoved the last bit of hot dog into her mouth. Abby didn't answer but dragged her away. "Come on, apparently there's a lot of cute guys there."

Hearing this, Clarissa dropped her drink into the nearest garbage can and they hurried off together.

CHAPTER EIGHT

"WOW, YOU'VE GOT CURVES!"

Clarissa looked at Abby in the change room mirror. She'd insisted they buy new swimsuits before going to the cute-boys-beach. Abby couldn't find any full swimsuits she liked. The selection was few and picked over, but there were plenty of bikini options.

She was now standing in front of the change room mirror wearing a bikini Clarissa had picked out for her. She didn't look half bad. Her waist was petite, her breasts small but firm, and a little belly showed above the bikini bottoms. All in all it didn't look nearly as bad as she'd feared, in fact, she looked kind of sexy.

Clarissa shook her head. "So that's what you've been hiding under those granny clothes you like to wear. What a waste."

"Yes, well, they're my curves," Abby said to her. "And I have no intention of sharing them with anyone."

Clarissa gave Abby a curious look. "Who said anything about sharing them?"

Abby's cheeks flared. "I didn't."

"With whom would you be sharing them?"

"No one."

"Well, you know what?" Clarissa whispered, leaning in as though sharing a big secret. "I saw a little two year old on the beach today in a bikini. If a toddler can wear one, then I'm pretty sure you can handle wearing one."

Abby rolled her eyes. "I guess it does look better than my old swimsuit."

"That wasn't a swimsuit. That was armor."

* * *

Lake Skaha Beach was bigger and felt hotter than Okanagan Beach, even though they were only a ten minute drive from each other. Every inch of sand was covered in beach towels with swimsuit clad tourists tanning in the sun. Abby's heart sank when she saw how many people there were. She'd never find Jade amongst all these people.

Clarissa had gone to the washroom nearby to fix her hair so Abby walked over to a colourful vendor tent by the concession area, needing to get out of the sun. The tent had all the typical beach accessories for sale: sunglasses, hats, friendship bracelets and anklets. Abby stopped to look at the jewelry.

Shell necklaces swayed in the breeze coming off the water, clinking together melodiously. She took a white shell in her hand and inspected it. It had a brown swirl at the center and felt cool and smooth to touch. It was beautiful.

"Did you want to buy that necklace?" someone said from behind her.

"No, thank you, I don't have any cash with..." Abby's swim bag slipped from her grasp and landed by her feet when she turned to see who it was. Jade leaned over and picked up the bag for her. Just when she'd given up looking, he was here, and once again he was shirtless and wore only swim shorts.

"I wasn't sure I'd see you again," he said, "after you ran off last night. You never told me your name."

Before she could reply, Clarissa appeared, looking angry. She snatched the bag from Jade's grasp. "Is this kid bothering you, Abby?" she said, glaring at him.

Jade stepped back in surprise.

"No," Abby said quickly, then couldn't think of anything else to say.

Jade looked from Abby to Clarissa then back again. "It was nice to meet you... Abby. Maybe I'll see you around." He gave her a little salute, then turned and walked away.

She wanted to call him back, but what would she say?

"What was he doing with your bag?" Clarissa asked. "Was he bothering you? You look freaked out or something."

"No, I just dropped it."

"Stay away from those college kids, they're bad news."

* * *

"I put the SPF sixty sunblock on you Abby, quit worrying," Clarissa mumbled into her towel. It was half an hour later and they were on the beach sun tanning. Clarissa turned her head to the side to look at Abby, who was also laying on a towel in her new bikini. "Just turn onto your back, it's been a half hour."

"I can't, it's too embarrassing."

Clarissa sighed and got up. "You seriously need to lighten up girl. I'm going into the water."

Abby's heart sank as she watched her friend walk off. *Why am I always disappointing everyone? Including myself. Why can't I just let go?* She was an adult now and could do whatever she wanted, so why couldn't she just relax?

Abby forced herself to get up, exposing her bikini clad body to the world. *Nobody is looking at you. This isn't small town Alberta. Bikinis are okay here. My body is okay, it's not embarrassing.* She repeated the last line over in her mind until she relaxed and a smile formed on her lips. She'd come here to enjoy herself and that's exactly what she would do. Her skin tingled beneath the warm sun and she looked out across the water.

If only Clarissa hadn't been so rude to Jade. She didn't like younger guys. Every guy she'd set Abby up with had been at least ten years older.

Abby walked towards the water. The hot sand burned her feet and she quickly ran to the water's edge, maneuvering between the towels and sunbathers. She spotted Clarissa sitting on the dock, showcasing her model figure to the guys who were in the water talking to her.

Then she spotted Jade down the beach and her breath caught. Why did she become instantly nervous whenever she saw him? He was playing Frisbee with a group of friends. One of the girls giggled when she missed catching the Frisbee.

Abby's chest tightened as she watched Jade. Why was she so taken by him? It wasn't like her. The girls tried to get his attention by acting dramatic and being loud, but Jade ignored their antics, tossing the Frisbee to another guy. Abby smiled.

If she were a different person she'd run over and join them, but she couldn't. She was plain and boring Abby, always cautious and slightly socially inept.

Frowning, she headed back to her towel to cover up and get back into her clothes.

CHAPTER NINE

"NO, I TOLD YOU I was coming here with Abby," Clarissa yelled into her cell phone. They were back at the hotel room and it was evening now. "It's not my fault you were too drunk to understand... What? I did text you... When? I was SLEEPING. Yes, we went to bed before supper because we were so tired from the drive. Why would I lie?"

Abby waited patiently, pretending to busy herself with her own cell phone. It was getting late. Too hungry to wait any longer, she typed the words *going for supper* into a text box, then showed her phone to Clarissa. Clarissa stopped pacing long enough to read it and nod.

"My fault?" she yelled into the phone. "I never asked you to follow me here! That's what stalkers do... Yes, that's exactly it, Matt." Her tone became sarcastic.

"I didn't want you to see me flirting with all the guys on the beach. It's not like I'm here to be a good friend to Abby... WHAT? Who told you that?"

Abby quietly snuck out of the room and closed the door behind her. She breathed sigh of relief. The evening air was warm and welcoming. Poor Clarissa. She always ended up arguing with her boyfriends.

Abby headed down the sidewalk past the pirate themed restaurant and pub. It was too lively for her. Maybe there was a simple diner or sandwich place somewhere down the road.

A neon sign caught her attention. The words BEACH STORE shone bright above the doors. People came in and out holding ice cream cones and snacks. Abby headed in that direction.

There wasn't much for food in the Beach Store, other than ice-cream. She walked down the aisles, stopping to look at the T-shirts and sundresses. Even with all the money her parents had, she never got to buy frivolous things while on vacation, or any other time.

She ran her fingers along the light fabrics of the sundresses, wondering how they would feel to wear.

They were so pretty and fun. Getting material gifts from her parents wouldn't have made her feel more loved, would it? Yet there was something special about receiving a gift for no reason, just as a show of affection.

Come to think of it, Ben had never bought her anything, not even lunch, in their entire year of dating. He assumed she had lots of money because her parents were rich. She didn't bother to tell him that, other than a small living allowance, she refused to take her parents' money.

Abby let go of the soft fabric of the dress she'd been looking at and went down the next aisle. She stopped at a display of Ogopogo stuffed toys and picked one up. They looked like a cross between a snake and a dragon. She took two of them and continued on through the store, picking up things that interested her.

When she reached the front counter her arms were full.

"How will you be paying?" the cashier asked as she began to ring in the items. Abby hesitated. The words 'with my parents' money' came to her mind.

"I'm sorry, I just realized I don't have my bank card with me," Abby lied, feeling sheepish.

"No problem." The lady scooped up the pile, pulling it off the counter. Abby frowned.

"Wait." She grabbed one of the Ogopogos. "I have some change for this one."

It was just a small gift to herself but it made her feel happy.

The sky was dark when Abby stepped out of the store. She headed to the beach with her Ogopogo plush in hand. A warm breeze blew off the water, smelling like rain. She took off her sandals and walked along the shore. The cool sand between her toes was becoming a familiar feeling now. She could live here for the rest of her life and be happy. But that wasn't going to happen. At some point she'd have to head back home and figure her life out.

She stopped to look out over the water. A gentle breeze lifted her hair, freeing her neck and cooling her. Why hadn't she joined Jade in his Frisbee game on the beach? Or at least run over to ask for his number so they could meet up for lunch sometime? Her mother wasn't here now, stopping her from doing anything, and yet she still couldn't do something as simple as approach an attractive guy to ask for his number.

Abby's shoulders slumped. How would she ever work full time, get married, have kids and care for her own home if something as simple as getting a guy's phone number terrified her so much?

"Abby?"

Looking up, she saw Jade coming towards her and she almost dropped her Ogopogo plush toy.

"I thought you might show up here eventually," he said when he got closer. The pleased look in his eyes made Abby's heart skip. No one had ever looked so pleased to see her before.

"Were you waiting for me?" she asked, hugging her Ogopogo tight. "How'd you know I'd be here?"

"This is where we first met." Jade shrugged. He was wearing a black t-shirt with the name of some rock band on it and a light zip-up hoodie with black and red stripes.

"I hadn't even noticed it was the same spot," Abby said. Or had she? Wasn't she going to get supper? And yet she'd ended up here.

Jade looked down at the sand, putting his hands into his pockets.

"But I'm glad you're here." Abby added quickly, "I wanted to come say hi at the beach but you were playing Frisbee with some girls."

"It was a group with girls and guys," Jade said, a glint of humour in his eyes.

"Well, yes." Abby grinned. It was the girls that she'd noticed with him, because she was jealous that she wasn't one of them.

"Are you staying on this beach?" Jade asked.

"Yes."

"I'm staying at the other beach, with my parents."

"Oh, that's too bad."

"Yeah, I wish I was here on my own and not with my parents."

"I mean it's too bad that you're not staying on this beach."

"That too," Jade took his hands out of his pockets and moved in a bit closer.

"I can understand not wanting your parents around," Abby said.

"You came with your friend, the red haired girl?"

"Clarissa? Yes. She came with me actually. I was the one running away."

Jade smiled at this. "That's kind of what I'm doing right now." Abby gave him a worried look and he added, "I mean sneaking away from camp to come look for you."

"Oh," Abby said. "I'm glad you did."

He glanced down at her lips and a sudden warmth stirred inside of her. "Um," she cleared her throat. "Sorry about Clarissa. She doesn't like college boys."

"Then I guess it's a good thing I'm not in college."

Abby was about to ask how old he was when he put his hands onto her shoulders and turned her around to face to water. His touch was warm. "Close your eyes," he said.

"What? Why?"

"Just close your eyes."

Abby tensed but closed her eyes anyway, holding her Ogopogo tight.

Jade slipped something around her neck. The smooth object felt cool on her chest.

She opened her eyes and looked down. It was the shell necklace she'd been eyeing earlier that day at the vender tent.

She turned to Jade. "You bought it?"

He was closer than she expected when she turned so quickly and it caught her off guard. She stepped back and tripped on the uneven sand. Jade reached out to grab her.

"I'm okay," Abby insisted, catching her footing. She placed one hand on Jade's chest to keep him at arm's length, his light t-shirt warm against her hand. He picked up her Ogopogo stuffie which had fallen onto the sand.

"You found the gift shop Ogopogo toys," he said, dusting off the sand from the plush.

"Yes." Abby grabbed for it, but Jade lifted it away from her.

"I'm just looking at it," he said, a mischievous look in his eyes. Abby crossed her arms and waited as he inspected her special gift to herself.

"Can I have it back now?" she said, reaching for it again. She couldn't help but worry that he'd steal it from her, or wreck it somehow, which was silly but he did have a playful grin on his face as he backed away, holding the Ogopogo out of reach. Abby jumped for it and missed and then he ran away from her.

"Give it back!" Abby yelled, running after him. She almost caught the plush a few times, but he teased her with it and snatched it away at the last second each time.

Done with the game, she scooped her foot under Jade's legs and tripped him. He fell backward onto the sand, finally dropping the Ogopogo toy. Abby grabbed it and ran.

She would have ran back to the hotel if Jade hadn't caught her first. He was a faster runner than she was. She screamed when he caught up to her and laughed, a carefree laughter that didn't even sound like her. "Stop it," she said breathlessly. "It's mine."

Jade wrapped his arms around her to try and get the Ogopogo out of her hands but she leaned forward and he fell over her, then she ran again. This time he cornered her into the lake. Water splashed up around them, soaking the new sundress she'd bought along with the bikini that day.

At waist deep, Abby slowed down and so did Jade. He began coughing and she waited for him to catch his breath.

"Do you have a cold?" she asked.

"Something like that," he said. Then he splashed her.

"Stop," she laughed. "He'll get wet." She held her Ogopogo tight. Jade was suddenly close. His eyes caught the moonlight that glistened off the water. Abby wanted to be kissed, right at that moment, a real kiss like she'd seen in the movies, not a polite peck on the lips or a quick kiss followed by a pat on the shoulder, the way Ben had done. Clarissa kissed on first dates all the time. But this wasn't technically even a date. They'd just met.

"Are you okay?" Jade asked, reaching up to move her hair out of her face. "Sorry I splashed you."

"It's fine." Abby held her breath as Jade moved closer.

"Let's go put Oggy somewhere safe," he said, putting his arm around her and squeezing her shoulders in a friendly way. "Then would you like to go to the Fun Zone?"

His embrace warmed her and she leaned into him. "Okay, that would be fun."

* * *

Abby set Oggy on the bed and quickly went to get changed. Clarissa wasn't in the hotel room so she stopped to text her that she was going to the Fun Zone.

Her suitcase was open in the middle of the floor, clothes thrown everywhere. Clarissa had been rummaging through her stuff, looking for clothes to borrow. Abby dug through the pile near her suitcase. There wasn't much to choose from. Why hadn't she brought nicer clothes? Deciding on a simple black tank-top and jean shorts, she got changed quickly and went back outside.

Jade was still there, leaning against the banister and looking more attractive than ever, with his hair still wet and eyes bright.

He walked over and linked arms with her.

"Ready?"

"Yes." She hugged his arm tight. "Let's go."

CHAPTER TEN

JADE HELD ABBY'S HAND as they waited in line to get tickets at the Fun Zone Amusement Park. She couldn't keep up with his touches, there were too many to constantly reject, and his confidence made it impossible to say no, so she let him hold her hand. His fingers were interlaced with hers.

The Fun Zone was even more magical in the evening than in the day. Many lights filled the night with bright colours and Tropical looking plants gave the place an island paradise feel to it. The smell of rain hung in the air and thunder rolled in the distance.

Jade paid for their tickets when it was their turn and then they headed into the park, passing by the mini golf area. Abby almost suggested they play a round, but Jade was already heading for the rides.

"Where to first?" he asked.

His thumb made slow circles on the back of Abby's hand.

"I don't know," Abby blinked, feeling dazed. She looked around at all the rides. "When do they close?"

"Eleven. So we don't have too much time." Jade's expression became serious.

"What's wrong?"

"Nothing. How about... the bumper boats?"

Abby turned to where Jade was looking. A group of kids that had just finished their turn on the boats were now climbing out, soaking wet.

"I don't want to get wet again, I just got changed."

"What about those?" Jade pointed to a bungee apparatus that was bouncing kids high into the air while they were strapped into a harness.

"No thanks," Abby said.

"The Aerial Park then?" Jade pointed up.

Abby shook her head. "I'm terrified of heights."

"You can't be scared of everything."

Abby tensed but didn't reply.

"Come on, you only live once."

"Okay." Abby nodded. "You're right, let's try… that." She nodded to the aerial park above them.

"Awesome." Jade winked at her and let go of her hand to go get in line.

Abby avoided looking down as she climbed the wooden steps of the Aerial Park, an obstacle course high up in the air. Jade was somewhere above. It had taken her a lot longer to get into the harness and make her way up the steps than it had him. She had no idea where he was now and was too scared to look up. She definitely wouldn't be going up to the third level, which was the highest. The first level was scary enough.

A kid moved in front of her when she reached the intersection to the first level obstacles. He budded in to get to the rope bridge first. Abby almost lost her balance and tightened her hold on the safety rope.

The rope bridge seemed the safest obstacle. It had ropes on either side to hold onto. She stepped out and the bridge wobbled. Her stomach tightened but she continued forward.

At the middle of bridge Abby looked down, which was a mistake. Her foot slipped and her body swung out to the side. Screaming, she grasped her safety rope with both hands so tight that her knuckles were white. Why hadn't Jade waited for her so they could go together?

"Abby?" She heard him calling from somewhere high above, but she couldn't look up. It was just as terrifying as looking down.

The rope bridge wobbled again and she shut her eyes tight. Someone was on it with her now, hopefully a staff member coming to take her down. A moment later she felt arms wrap around her waist.

"Jade?" Abby turned and was suddenly in Jade's arms.

"You look terrified," he said.

"I am." She relaxed a little, feeling safer with his arms around her.

"Look," Jade whispered, close to her ear. He turned her slowly and she looked out over the horizon. The lights of the S.S. Sicamous twinkled down below and the lake spread out behind it.

A flash of lightning lit up the dark clouds above the waters. The view was breathtaking. Abby settled into Jade's embrace and he tightened his arms around her.

"Hey, you guys need to come down!" a staff member called up to them. "It's going to rain. We're closing the Aerial Park."

Jade turned Abby around and held her hand as they made their way back across the rope bridge and down the wooden steps. Though it had been terrifying, Abby would do it all again to feel Jade's arms around her once more.

A light rain fell as they walked away from the Fun Zone, hand in hand.

"How about we do mini golf next time," Jade said.

"Okay." Abby slowed her pace. Jade was falling behind. The drizzle was turning into a downpour as they made their way through the parking lot. People ran to their vehicles for cover, but Jade walked slowly.

"Are you okay?" Abby asked, remembering that he'd been coughing earlier.

"Just tired," he said.

The wind blew large rain drops against Abby's face and it was hard to hear Jade over the splash of rain on the concrete.

"Are you in a hurry to take cover?" he asked.

"No," Abby said. They walked on towards the beach, the rain soaking them through. The downpour settled into a gentle rain again, but the beach was now deserted. Lightning flashed above and thunder rolled. Abby shivered.

"Do you want to get out of the rain?" Jade asked.

"No. I love it. My mom would always rush me inside if we ever got caught in the rain. I wanted to stay and let it pour over me, even if I was freezing cold. But she never let me. She'd say, 'you'll catch your death'. That scared me when I was little. Then when I was seven or eight I finally realized she wasn't being literal."

"We can stay in the rain as long as you like," Jade said, pulling Abby closer to his side.

"Wow, look at the waves." Abby snuggled in close and Jade put his arm around her.

"It's almost scary," he said.

The waves crashed to the shore then spread out across the sand, reaching to their feet.

"Let's go in!" Abby clapped her hands together.

"What?" Jade gave her a questioning look. "Are you serious?"

"Yes!" She freed herself from his arms and took off her sandals. She was finally starting to let go and be spontaneous, why stop now? She'd climbed up on a scary aerial park, let herself get drenched in a downpour, swam in a lake and let Jade hold her hand when she'd only just met him.

Abby left her sandals behind and ran towards the water. The wave retreated back to the lake and then the next wave came.

"Abby!" Jade ran after her, his voice barely audible in the wind.

For a second, fear gripped her chest, then the next moment water was all around her and she was free. It wasn't even cold. The rain that had drenched her was much colder. A wave lifted her up and she laughed out loud at the thrill of it. Jade was in the water now too, but each time a wave rose up she lost sight of him.

A clap of thunder split the air and Abby screamed.

"Jade?" she called out. An oncoming wave caught her by surprise and went over her head. She surfaced, sputtering.

Jade appeared at her side. "You okay?"

"Yeah," she coughed.

"Let's get out of the water."

"No, I love this!"

"It's dangerous." Jade pulled her close.

"Now who's being a scaredy cat?" Abby pushed him into the water and he let himself be dunked. Surfacing, he grabbed her around the waist.

"Come on Abby. You'll catch your death."

"Very funny." Abby pushed against him to free herself but he held her tight, lifting her up into the next wave. It knocked them both over and their bodies collided.

"We should go," Jade said, moving away from her. "Or I might be the one to catch my death in this cold." Another wave washed them closer to shore and Abby got out of the water.

Back at the hotel, under the cover of the overhead balcony, Abby stood in front of her door, waiting. Jade looked distracted. He strummed his fingers on the banister that he was leaning against.

"Do you need a ride?" Abby asked. Why wasn't he leaving?

"No." His blue eyes studied her for a moment. "I have car. I can drive."

Abby nodded. A slight breeze blew over her and she shivered.

"How old are you anyway, twenty-four, twenty-five?" Jade asked.

"Me?" Abby laughed. "No."

"Twenty-three?"

"Don't try and flatter me." Abby crossed her arms.

"Twenty-One?" Jade asked.

"Stop it."

"Sorry." He put his hands up in surrender. "My older sister is twenty-six and you look younger than her so I was just wondering."

"How old are you?" Abby asked.

Jade shrugged. "Old enough."

"Well I know you're younger than me."

"How do you know? I could be twenty-five."

Abby laughed, but then stopped when she saw his hurt expression. "I just mean most guys my age are pretty boring and focused on their careers," she said. "But you're fun and energetic."

"So are you."

Jade stopped strumming the banister with his fingers and clasped it tight instead.

"So..." Abby hugged her arms around herself. "Your parents must have noticed that you're missing by now."

"Probably." Jade looked out at the beach on the other side of the street. "But I'm starting to get tired of always doing everything my dad tells me to. And of all the rules. They just don't seem to matter now."

Abby nodded. "My mom is so controlling too."

"Really?"

"Yes. It doesn't end when you're older, they still try and control your life."

"That sucks." Jade pushed away from the banister and came closer. "So is your controlling mom okay with your coming on this vacation?"

"She doesn't even know I'm here. She'd flip out."

Jade looked down at her as though trying to decide something. Another breeze blew over her wet clothes and she shivered again.

"You should get inside," Jade said, looking down at her lips. Abby took a half step back. He reached out and grasped a handful of her hair, squeezing some water out of it. "I wish I wasn't camping all the way at Skaha."

"Yeah."

"Can I see you again tomorrow?"

Abby nodded.

Jade slipped his hand behind her neck and leaned in to kiss her. She drew back and he stopped, letting his hand drop.

"Sorry."

"No, it's okay." Abby cleared her throat, confused. Why had she pulled away? True she'd only known Jade for one day but she would have really enjoyed that kiss. Now he'd probably never try again.

Jade ran his fingers through his hair, lifting it out of his face.

"I'll see you tomorrow," he said. Then he left.

CHAPTER ELEVEN

THE SHRILL OF HER CELL PHONE ringing woke Abby from a sound sleep, disrupting the peaceful rhythm of the rain drumming against the hotel window. It was open slightly and the fresh smell of rain drifted into the room.

Abby grabbed her phone and looked at it. The call display said 'Mom.' Were they back from their anniversary cruise already? There was no point in ignoring the call, her mom would just keep calling back.

Abby swiped the phone screen. "Hello?"

"You know how I disapprove of sleeping in. I don't see why you can't be up early, as a habit," her mother said. It wasn't the best greeting to wake up to.

"Hi Mom, how was the cruise?"

"You'll need to be getting up early once you're married, making Ben's breakfast before he heads off to work. Unless he hires a live-in maid. But I don't recommend it in your first year of marriage."

Abby rubbed her forehead. A headache was coming on.

"I think it should be a fall wedding," her mom continued. "Of this year. I was thinking, when the children come, a nice private school would be best for them. I always regretted putting you through the public system. I suppose we weren't as wealthy back then, and now your father owns half the town. Did Ben talk to you about the shareholders meeting—?"

"Mom, slow down!"

"Well, I called to tell you to wear your nice dress suit to the party."

"What par—?"

"Your father's inviting everyone. It will be a great business mingling opportunity. The relatives are coming too of course, except your Cousin Rodney and Uncle Cassey, thank goodness. They always make a scene."

"Oh, you're 35th Anniversary Party." Abby sighed. She'd completely forgotten.

"Of course, what party did you think I was talking about?"

"Mom, if so many people are coming to your party then I'm sure you won't really miss me if I don't come, right?"

Her mom laughed. "Of course I would! We both missed you very much while we were away on this dreadful cruise. I know this is the first time we've been away from you for so long, but your father insisted."

"No, that's not what I meant."

"Anyway, I haven't been able to get a hold of Ben. Busy with his paperwork I suppose. But with everyone coming to the party your father and I think it would be the perfect time to announce your engagement."

"What? Ben and I aren't—"

"Now don't interrupt me, Abby, I know what you're going to say. You're worried that your engagement announcement will overshadow your father and my 35th anniversary ceremony. But don't worry, it will only add to the celebration."

Abby put her mother on speaker phone, turning the volume down as low as it would go. She checked her text messages. Nothing from Ben, two from Clarissa.

She wrote Ben first, letting her mother go on and on about the party.

Text my mom and tell her we're not actually engaged or getting married. Thanks.

Then she read Clarissa's texts,

I'm heading back to AB. I tried 2 call u. Matt showed up to take me back. A waitress quit so he needs me 2 take extra shifts this weekend. Sorry. He's a jealous freak. Keep me updated.

Then another message, sent hours later.

We stopped at a BnB, too much driving. So romantic here! Hope u r ok.

Abby replied,

I'm fine. Parents' 35th anniversary party this weekend. I don't want to go.

"Abby? Are you listening?"

"Yes, Mom."

"Good, then don't forget. And I need the van back. Your father and I have decided to buy you an SUV, as a wedding gift. We're going tomorrow to pick it up…

Where are you dear? I'm driving by your apartment and I don't see the van parked out front."

"I left...with Clarissa."

"I hope she's paying you for all the gas you use driving her around all the time. I don't see why one of her boyfriends can't give her rides. Oh I have to go dear, there's a police car up ahead. I will see you on Saturday."

Abby hung up the phone and dragged herself out of bed. She packed her bags slowly, in no rush to leave. But it was time to go home.

After checking out of the hotel and having breakfast at a small diner, she drove down the Okanagan beachside road, taking in all the sights, not wanting to forget any part of this magical place.

The way home was in the direction of Skaha Lake, so she took a little detour to the beach there. Sun bathers were already setting out their umbrellas for the day. New venders were setting up their tents and bouncy castles lay on the grassy field in the park, across from the beach. Was there some kind of festival this weekend?

Abby pulled into a parking spot near the park. She couldn't spare too much time if she wanted to be back to Alberta by tomorrow night, but she could stop for a few minutes. Who knew when she'd see this place again, if ever.

The sun was warm on Abby's shoulders when she stepped out of the van. It would be another hot day.

The smell of the beach was now becoming familiar to her and she already missed the place. But she couldn't run away from home forever and pretend her parents didn't exist. As long as she was alive, she'd have a responsibility to them.

Abby headed for the beach, walking across the park. Kids were swarming the bouncy castles and a DJ at the beer gardens was spinning loud club music. Abby passed by the stage at the center of the park where a folk band was doing a sound check.

This would be a fun weekend for those who got to stay here. Abby frowned and reached up to touch the shell necklace that Jade had bought for her. Then, by some strange act of fate, she saw him.

He was playing with a little girl of about ten. Her dark hair and features suggested that they were probably related. He chased after her in a game of tag. Abby didn't want to interrupt them. It was enough to see Jade one last time. She smiled and closed her eyes a moment, capturing the image of his playful expression in her mind.

"Abby!" She heard his voice and opened her eyes. He waved and ran over. The dark haired girl ran off with two other girls her age to one of the bouncy castles.

"You found me!" Jade called as he hurried over. He stopped when he reached Abby, putting his hand to his chest, catching his breath.

"I did." Abby said. "Are you camping with your family?"

"Yes," he looked back at the bouncy castles. "Well, I'm not camping with them. I'm with a group. That's my little cousin." Jade pointed behind him. "She's visiting for the Peach Festival and staying with my parents at the campground. Want to try the bouncy castles?" Jade took her hand.

"No, I can't stay," Abby pulled back.

"Stay, please," Jade said, pulling her close. "We don't have to do the festival stuff. I'm actually too tired for it anyway."

"I'm sorry, I can't," Abby said, keeping him at arm's length.

"Sure you can," Jade put his hands on her waist.

"I'm serious," Abby frowned.

"I'm serious too, spend the day with me."

"What about your family, or your group?"

"They won't miss me," Jade said. "Come, let me buy you a snow cone."

"Okay," Abby gave in. "But just for a little bit."

Jade put his arm around her and led her to the vender tents.

They passed the kids' karaoke corner, which was bustling with tweens. Jade stopped to listen to the two girls singing on the stage. He cheered when they finished their song.

"Wait here," he said, letting go of Abby's hand. He made his way through the crowd and had a word with the sound technician, who nodded in agreement.

Jumping up on stage, he grabbed the microphone and removed it from its stand.

"This song goes out to the beautiful Abby," he said, pointing her out in the crowd.

All heads turned in Abby's direction and for a moment a familiar dread, of being stared at in a crowd of people, gripped her. But when she looked back to Jade on the stage, the other faces faded away. He winked at her, then nodded to the sound guy, who then started the music.

At the very first note a chorus of squeals rose up from the tween girls in the crowd. Abby recognized the song too, which had been playing on the radio all summer.

"Baby let me take you out tonight," Jade sang. "We can go anywhere that you'd like..."

Abby laughed, then covered her mouth with her hand. It was so sweet. No one had ever serenaded her before. Jade danced along to the song, riling up the crowd of young girls.

"Tell me where you want to go, we'll take it slow, I'll give you anything that you want, I'll give you every part of my heart, baby don't say no, don't say no."

Jade looked right at her and Abby's cheeks flushed. He had a great singing voice but couldn't hit the high notes, which made the performance all the more endearing.

"Please tell me you..." he struggled to reach the high note, which set off a cheer from the girls. "Tell me that you want me too. And if you do. Can I kiss you?" Jade jumped off the stage. He made his way to Abby. "Tell me you, you want me too. And if you do. Can I kiss you? Can I kiss you?"

Abby's cheeks were ablaze. She fought the urge to run away and hide as Jade got closer. He took her hand in his, then leaned in and gave her a quick kiss on the cheek. He was about to hug her when something caught his attention in the distance. Abby turned to see where he was looking but she couldn't tell.

Jade went back to the stage and passed the mic to a group of young girls who continued singing the chorus of the song. Then he returned to Abby, embracing her in a spinning hug that lifted her feet off the ground. She laughed out loud at the wonderful sensation of being swept up into his arms.

"I have to go," he said in her ear, "meet me at the Sicamous later."

"Jade I can't..." Abby said. But he was already gone, hurrying through the crowd before she could catch him. She wanted to say a proper goodbye, but in the end, there was no use in dragging it out. They'd never be together. And there couldn't have been a more perfect way to remember Jade.

Abby closed her eyes, wrapped her arms around herself, savouring the moment. When she opened her eyes, she knew it was time to go home.

CHAPTER TWELVE

"ABBY'S STOMACH TURNED, threatening to upheave the bland icing of her parents' anniversary cake. All evening it had been the same discussion with every friend of her parents, with every cousin and aunt. They wanted to know what she was 'doing' now, if she was married or travelling or working, what her plans were for the future. She'd avoided any direct answers and simply smiled, avoiding the reality that she was, in fact, doing nothing with her life at the moment.

Now, finally, the mandatory greetings and small-talk were over with and she was enjoying a brief moment of peace at the dessert table. It lasted about all but thirty seconds.

"Can't decide?" someone asked from beside her. Abby looked up at the tall, thirty-something man with brown hair, wearing a nice suit. Yet another person she did not know at this party. He had a confident stance and kind eyes. Judging by his expensive suit, Abby guessed he was a business associate of her father's, high up in the commercial real estate business.

He offered his hand in a handshake. "Charles."

"Abby," she said, taking his hand. She waited for him to ask her what she did for a living that made her worthy of inhabiting this planet, but he didn't ask.

"Try the Nanaimo bars," he said instead. "Can't go wrong with those."

"Oh, I couldn't eat another bite after that cake," Abby said. "I was just standing here trying to figure out if I can still fit under this table."

Charles laughed.

"I used to climb under the dessert table," Abby continued, "when my parents had dinner parties, and eat desserts with my imaginary friend." Why was she opening up to a stranger? Had she become more social since meeting Jade? Or was it because Charles didn't seem to have an agenda for being here, like everyone else did.

"You look like you could use an imaginary friend right about now," Charles said, grabbing a Nanaimo bar. Abby smiled, a real smile for the first time tonight. She could use a friend at the moment, a real one. Before she could reply, she felt a tap on her shoulder. Ben stood behind her, looking chipper.

"Ben? I thought you were in Ontario," she said.

Charles nodded politely at them, taking his leave without a word. Abby felt a twinge of disappointment.

"I took an early flight back," Ben said. "It didn't seem right to miss your parents' anniversary party."

Abby narrowed her eyes at him. He was up to something.

"You got my text right?" she asked him.

"I did and I've been thinking," Ben looked around then lowered his voice, "I'll agree to your condition for getting married."

Abby was too dumbstruck to reply.

"Listen, I can't be the majority shareholder in your father's company without Canadian Citizenship and my parents won't hand over their shares until I'm married," Ben continued.

"But... my father is majority shareholder."

"It's either me or these other guys offering to buy the whole thing and if they do, your parents lose everything. At least with me we can keep it all in the family."

Abby swallowed hard. What was he trying to say? "My mom still has the cleaning business."

"Well it definitely won't afford her current lifestyle, or yours."

"I don't live a lavish lifestyle." Abby's hands formed into fists at her sides.

"You don't work either," Ben continued on before she could give an angry reply. "Just think about it, okay?"

"So you'd agree to my terms," Abby asked, "just to get the company?"

"Yes, as long as you agree to let me work out a solution for myself."

"Solution?" Abby's brows furrowed. "What kind of solution? I don't understand."

"Did you hear? My dad bought a chain of McDonald's restaurants." Ben was no longer whispering but talking loudly, smiling and looking around the room.

"What?" Before Abby could say any more Ben pulled her to the microphone nearby that was set up for the speeches during supper.

He tilted the mic to his mouth and spoke into it. "Excuse me everyone, if I could have your attention, please."

The chatter in the room died down to a soft lull.

"Ben, don't," Abby said in a loud whisper, but he ignored her. She spotted her parents at the back of the room. Her mom gave her a tiny wave. A sea of faces stared back at her as she looked out over the crowd. Her vision spun for a moment, then her ears began to ring, so loudly that she couldn't hear what Ben was saying into the microphone. What was he doing? He knew she felt trapped and disoriented in crowds.

Ben got down on one knee and slipped a ring onto her shaky finger. Applause erupted around the room. People moved in close, pulling Abby into a hug, one after another. A pounding in her ears drowned out their words. *No, I don't want this.*

She began counting in her head, something that she'd learned to do to cope in stressful situations. One to ten then start at one again. Somewhere in the back of her mind she pictured the lights of the Sicamous, reflecting off the dark waters of the Okanagan Lake at night. And she imagined herself swimming in the cool waves, away from everything and everyone. Everyone but Jade.

CHAPTER THIRTEEN

"I STILL DON'T UNDERSTAND why you didn't just say no and walk out of there," Clarissa said around a mouthful of donut. They were drowning their sorrows in coffee and pastries at a donut shop. Clarissa had broken up with Matt after she'd caught him looking through all of her text messages while she was in the shower.

"I had a bit of a panic attack I think. I don't know. That hasn't happened in years," Abby said, playing with the colourful sprinkles on her plate. "I'm just glad I didn't faint or something."

"I should have come to the party," Clarissa sighed. "I should have been there for you. Then this would have never happened."

"I was up all night thinking about it. This engagement could be my chance to grow up. No one else is ever going to agree to... to what I asked Ben to agree to. I could finally get married, and start my life."

"You don't know that there isn't someone else out there who—"

"You said it yourself." Abby looked at her friend. "No man would agree to marry me on the condition that we'd never have sex."

"So why did Ben agree then?"

To get Canadian Citizenship. But she couldn't tell Clarissa that. She already knew what Clarissa would say, and it wouldn't be very lady-like.

Abby frowned down at her uneaten sprinkle donut. Would her father really lose his company if Ben didn't buy out the shares from his parents and become majority shareholder? Or was Ben just being dramatic. "I don't know," Abby finally said.

Clarissa set down her pastry. "What did he say again? About agreeing to your condition of marriage if you agreed to his condition?"

"Solution. He said as long as I agree to let him work out his own solution."

"That sounds fishy to me."

"But it doesn't matter anyway. Don't you see? In two months I could be married, have a new house and my own car, and no longer be living off my parents." *And my dad's company would still be in the family.*

"No, but you'd be living off Ben," Clarissa said.

"I give up." Abby's voice rose as she fought back tears. She pushed her chair back and stood up.

"Wait," Clarissa said, standing up as well. "I'm sorry I said that."

"What am I supposed to do Clarissa?" Abby said, her tears threatening to fall. "I'm never going to get an offer like this again and, as you've probably noticed, I'm not exactly capable of being independent."

"I think you are."

Abby let out a sigh and sat back down. "Ben isn't all bad. He's a bit immature." She shook her head. "Imagine me being the one to say that he's immature. He's got a job and knows how to socialize—"

"That doesn't make him mature." Clarissa sat down too, this time she took the chair next to Abby rather than the one across the table.

She put a hand on Abby's shoulder. "It's up to you. I know girls who have settled for much worse."

Abby laughed. "Thanks. That makes me feel a lot better."

"I also know girls who chased after true love and were miserable in the end anyway. Life is complicated and nobody ever said it would be easy. There's no shame in catching a break once in a while. I just think you should do what makes you happy."

"It would make my parents happy."

"Yes. But would it make you happy?"

Abby thought about this for a moment. "Before the engagement announcement, I was having a horrible time at the party. Everyone was asking me what I'm doing these days, and I felt like I've been on pause, done nothing at all. Then after Ben proposed in front of everyone, it's like they were all proud of me, congratulating me and—"

"But would marrying Ben make *you* happy?"

"...and it made me happy. I felt better about myself, like I could belong, and fit in with everyone else." Abby looked down at the diamond ring on her finger. "Making other people happy, like my parents and you and..." she almost said 'Jade' but then stopped herself, "Making others happy, is what makes me happy."

Clarissa gave her a hug then got up. "Then I will support you in whatever you decide. So does this mean we'll get to go wedding dress shopping together?"

"Possibly?" Abby smiled. She felt a twinge of excitement at the thought. "Seeing as I'm engaged and all." She held up her hand with the diamond ring.

"So then, no more running away?"

"Nope. I'm finally ready to move forward," Abby said with a certainty that she didn't feel.

"Well, you're better off with Ben than I am with my hundredth break-up, and counting."

"No one's got it easy, do they?"

Clarissa grabbed the last bite of Abby's donut and ate it. "Nope."

CHAPTER FOURTEEN

ABBY GATHERED UP HER piles of sketch paper on her drawing desk. The hours and years of work they represented was depressing. At one time in her life she used to look at her comic pages and feel like they were destined for great things.

She imagined she would fulfill her dream of becoming a graphic artist and having her own comic series. But now all she saw was what her mother saw; a complete waste of time and energy.

She piled the papers carefully together and slipped them into a box. One benefit of being a home-maker to a husband who could support her was that she could continue working on things like her drawing. Yet the thought didn't cheer her up for some reason.

She was about to close the box when she noticed a comic strip she'd drawn the previous year. The girl superhero she had created could command the lakes and rivers, the clouds and the rain. The boy in the comic, who wasn't a superhero yet had hidden powers of his own, looked a lot like Jade.

Abby smiled at the coincidence. It was the hair. If she changed a few details she could make him look just like Jade.

"Abby," Clarissa whispered, poking her head into the room. "Red Alert!"

Abby closed the box and a second later her mother came in.

"I see you're almost done. Good. I'd like to have you moved in by tonight. We're having some friends over and I don't want boxes sitting out in front of the house. Why don't we put all this stuff into the garage instead?"

For a second Abby thought her mom had said the 'garbage' instead of the 'garage'. Either way it would have made her feel the same, like her stuff didn't matter, like she didn't matter. She pushed the thought aside. Her mom just wanted what was best. There was no denying that she cared for Abby, and her future. Maybe she cared a little too much.

"It will be moved into your new house with Ben in a few months anyway." Her mom smiled. Then she seemed to remember something and pulled out an envelope from her purse. "I was just at the office checking in with Sharon and she gave me this." She handed Abby the envelope. "It's addressed to you. It came to the cleaning office."

Abby looked at the return address. *Skaha Lake Campground.*

"Thanks." She quickly tucked the letter away.

"Someone you know?" her mother asked.

"Well, I do have a friend camping in B.C. right now." Abby turned back to her box. "I should get more packing done though, if you want me moved in before supper."

"Do you need any help? I can call one of the maids from the office."

"No, it's okay. Clarissa's helping me."

Abby's mom leaned into the room, her brows furrowed. "She's moving in with that man, and they're not even married." She shook her head. "Maybe you should talk to her."

"Mom, Clarissa knows what she's doing." Abby spotted Clarissa in the hallway behind her mom, rolling her eyes and making faces. She held back a chuckle. Clarissa had gotten back together with Matt in the past few days and they were now moving in together. Whether or not it was a good idea was Clarissa's business. "Don't worry about her Mom," Abby said. "You do enough worrying about me."

"That's true." Her mom straightened up and smiled. "Well, I'm off to see your father. It will be nice to have you back in the house again, even if it is just for a little while."

"Okay, bye." Abby waved her off, anxious to get at the envelope she held behind her back. She strummed her fingers on it as she waited to hear the front door close. When it finally did, she ripped open the envelope. The letter was from Jade. It read,

Abby, The Tiki Shores Resort said you checked out. I remembered the company name on your van and called the Alberta

office. They wouldn't give me your number but I hope this letter reaches you. (Hope you don't mind). Call me?

At the bottom of the letter was a phone number.

"Abby?" Clarissa looked into the room. "Are you alright?"

"Yes." Abby tucked the letter under her pillow. "I'm fine."

"You look like you're about to cry."

"No, I was just... Everything is changing kind of fast, that's all."

"Tell me about it!" Clarissa sighed, coming into the room to sit on Abby's bed. "Sorry that you have to move out. Like I said, I can continue paying the other half of the rent, even if I'm living with Matt now. I don't mind."

"No," Abby shook her head. "That wouldn't be fair. And it's okay. I don't mind going home. It's only for a short while."

"This is what you wanted, right? To be engaged before you turned thirty? Are you going to have an engagement party?"

"Oh... I'm not sure." Abby got up and pulled clothes out of her closet. "I've got a lot of packing to do, so..."

"I can tell something's wrong." Clarissa crossed her arms. "I'm your best friend, remember?"

Abby didn't reply. She pulled a red dress off of its hanger and her diamond engagement ring caught on the sheer lining, ripping it.

"Shit," Abby said under her breath.

Clarissa's eyebrows shot up. "Wow, that's the first time I've ever heard you swear." She gave Abby a concerned look but didn't ask any more questions. "I'll leave you to it then. But let me know if you need any help, I don't have a deadline to be all packed up by supper time, like you do. My stuff can wait."

Abby nodded, then turned away. "Thanks Clarissa, but I think I just need to be alone right now."

CHAPTER FIFTEEN

ABBY DREAMED OF THE OKANAGAN, its waters raging with waves in a storm. Rain fell in a downpour. Jade was waiting for her outside the S.S. Sicamous museum doors but she couldn't get to him. She called to him from across the road but the downpour had caused a large river to form on the street between them and he couldn't hear her call to him.

He continued to wait, but there was no getting across. Then he checked his watch, waved goodbye and left.

"No, wait! Jade!" Abby woke with a start, drenched in a cold sweat as though she actually *had* been out in a rainstorm. The clock on the bedside table said 3:11 AM. Her childhood bedroom felt smaller than ever, the four walls seemed to close in on her. The shelves of stuffed animals and teddy-bears were still there; gifts from friends, back when she still had birthday parties, before she was seven.

Abby got out of bed. She wouldn't get back to sleep now, not with the stuffed animals all staring at her, reminding her that she wasn't any better off in life than she'd been at age seven. She grabbed some clothes from her suitcase, then went to take a shower.

The full moon shined brightly, through the frosted glass window in the bathroom. It made Abby wish she was someone else, living in a world where magic and true romance existed. She showered quickly, not wanting to wake anyone. She would have enjoyed a longer shower but the brief one was enough to make her feel better.

Outside on the back patio the moon greeted her again, brightening the backyard. Abby stepped out with a cup of tea and her cell phone in hand. Jade's letter stuck out of her sweater pocket.

The air was crisp, but not too cold. She pulled her sweater closed at the front then sat down on a chair with a plush cushion. The grass smelled freshly cut this early in the morning. Its rich scent calmed her nerves.

Was it a bad idea to call Jade at this hour? She wouldn't get a chance to during the day, not with her mother in the house and Clarissa taking her dress shopping in the afternoon.

Abby turned on her cell phone and called Jade's number, dialing quickly before she could get too nervous and change her mind. It would bother her all day if she ignored the letter and didn't call him, at least to explain that she was engaged now and would not be returning to Penticton.

The phone rang only once before Jade picked it up. "Abby?" he said, his voice sounding rough with sleep.

Abby smiled. "How did you know it was me?"

"Wishful thinking I guess," Jade said. He sounded so close, like he was answering the call here in town and not many hours away. Abby looked up at the moon, wondering if Jade could see it too from where he was.

"I don't think I'll be coming back to Penticton," she said softly.

There was a pause, before Jade replied. "I'd like to hang out with you again."

Abby's smile grew even though she felt sad. "That's not really possible, because I'm in Alberta."

"If you tell me where in Alberta, I'll come to you."

"Jade... I'm engaged to be married."

There was another pause. Abby pulled her knees up close to her chest and hugged them.

"When's the wedding?" Jade asked.

"In a month, maybe two."

"Then we have four weeks, maybe more, to hang out."

Abby laughed softly but didn't reply.

"Unless you postpone the wedding," Jade continued, "until...like ten years from now?"

"I'll look into doing that," Abby said, playing with her hair.

"Seriously though, I want to come see you."

The fluttering in Abby's stomach was becoming more intense.

"Will you spend one more day with me?" Jade asked.

Abby rubbed her face with one hand, trying to think. Surely he was just flirting now and not serious. How would they manage the distance between them, just to spend one day together? She decided to play along.

"Sure," she said.

"I can't stop thinking about you."

Abby gripped her phone tighter. Was he just half asleep or something?

"Are you sure you want to drive all the way here just for a day?"

"I'd do it even for an hour with you."

Abby laughed. "Your parents won't be happy about it."

"I'm tired of doing what they want."

Me too. Abby closed her eyes. *But I'm not strong enough to take my life into my own hands.* "I'll be here," she said, her desire to see Jade growing with every minute she talked to him.

"Okay, should I meet you...at the Calgary Tower then?"

"That might not work. I'll be two hours south of the Calgary Tower, dress shopping with Clarissa most of the day. Sorry Jade." Abby's chest hurt. She wouldn't tell him where she lived. It didn't make sense for him to drive so far just to see her for one day. "It's late... It was nice to talk to you again."

"Okay. Thanks for calling," Jade said softly.

"Okay, bye."

"Goodbye Abby."

CHAPTER SIXTEEN

"**W**HY DON'T YOU COME OUT and we can have a look in the three-way mirror?" the saleswoman said over the changing stall. She had been assigned solely for Abby, which was rather unnecessary, since Clarissa was there to help.

"It's too big," Abby grumbled.

"All the dresses can be adjusted," the sales lady said in a chipper voice that sounded fake.

"It's really pretty." Clarissa finished tying the laces at the back of the dress and turned Abby around to look at her. "They can adjust the bust."

"Or I can stuff my bra." Abby stuck out her tongue at her friend. Clarissa laughed then opened the change room door.

Abby walked out and stepped up onto the raised platform in front of the large three-way mirror. Her breath caught when she saw her reflection.

She looked beautiful in the dress. Her neck was long and elegant, her waist tiny and her bust a soft olive colour against the lacey white bodice. The folds of the gown billowed out around her.

"Would you like to try another one?" the sales-lady asked.

Abby was too distracted to reply. Seeing herself in this fairytale dress made her dare to believe in happy endings. Would she be sacrificing her own happy ending if she married Ben? Did it matter? She could hardly be picky, not with her unrealistic conditions for marriage. Ben was more than sufficient for her, considering he was willing to agree to marry her.

Abby looked at Clarissa, standing quietly by her side. "Do you think I'm ready for this?"

"No one's ever ready for these big life steps," Clarissa said softly. "You just have to decide to do it, then jump in and hope for the best."

The saleslady left to go find another dress. Abby watched her in the mirror then her eyes stopped on an unexpected sight. It was Jade, dressed in jeans and a white dress shirt. He wore a silver suit jacket rolled up at the sleeves and unbuttoned at the front.

Abby shut her eyes tight and shook her head. She'd been up since three in the morning and now she was seeing things in mirrors.

"Abby," Clarissa whispered, pulling on her arm. "Isn't that the guy from the beach?"

Abby opened her eyes again, afraid to look. He was still there, leaning back against a mock pillar, arms crossed, admiring her in the mirror. She turned quickly, stepping off the platform and tripping on her dress in her eagerness to get to Jade. Clarissa caught her, looking from Jade to Abby then back again.

Abby freed herself and shuffled over to Jade as quickly as she could manage.

"Jade! What are you doing here? How did you find me?" She stopped in front of him, placing a hand against her chest to cover up the opening at the top of the bodice.

Jade took her free hand in his. The silver of his suit jacket brought out the blue in his eyes, and his dark hair looked midnight black compared to the white of his dress shirt.

"I found the city two hours south of Calgary and went to each bridal shop until I got to this one," Jade said. "You look amazing." His eyes travelled down over her.

Clarissa came up to them and took Abby's hand away from Jade's, then she pulled her back into the change room and closed the door.

"Is there something going on that you haven't told me about?" she whispered. "With *him*?"

"Not exactly," Abby said.

Clarissa crossed her arms. "Did you kiss him?"

Abby shook her head no.

"Did you do *more*?"

"What? NO! Why would I skip the kissing part and jump straight to more?"

"Then why is he here?"

"He wanted to spend one last day with me."

"Or one last night more likely."

Abby put her hands on her hips. "What do you mean? Do you think he'd only come if I gave him... something?"

"No, but..." Clarissa sighed. "You should just tell him to leave."

For once Abby didn't want to hear Clarissa's advice. She began to take off the dress. "Can you help me out of this dress?"

Clarissa helped and Abby changed back into her short sleeved blouse and khaki shorts.

"Do you want me to tell him to go?" Clarissa asked, handing Abby her shoes.

"No." Abby took the shoes and put them on. An irrational feeling gripped her; that Jade would disappear any second if she didn't hurry up.

Grabbing her cell phone off a chair, Abby ran out of the change room, then took Jade by the hand, leaving Clarissa and the elegantly carpeted store behind.

"I didn't mean to interrupt," Jade said once they were outside. "I can hang out while you try on dresses."

Abby slowed down as they put some distance between themselves and the bridal shop. "It's okay," she shrugged. "Those dresses are too beautiful for my wedding anyway."

Jade's brow furrowed. "What do you mean?"

"How long were you driving for?" Abby said, changing the subject. The sun warmed her bare arms and she was glad to be out of the air conditioning.

"About nine hours I think, and the time it took to visit the two other Bridal shops in town."

Abby stopped walking. "You've been driving since we got off the phone at three in the morning?" Just then her cell phone rang.

She glanced at the screen. It was her mother. "Sorry. I have to take this." She held back a sigh and answered the call. "Hello?"

"Sweetheart! I meant to be there today, I truly did," her mother said over the phone.

"It's okay."

"No, it's not okay. Don't pick a dress today. I want to be there when you pick a dress."

"Okay, I won't pick a dress today."

"Oh good," her mom sighed theatrically. "I need you to go to the house right away. You can browse dresses later. I was in such a rush this morning and your father's out of town, and Sofia isn't in to clean until later. I was in such a rush I forgot to feed Bailey. Poor girl, she's so sensitive in her old age, I'm afraid she will get depressed, having missed her breakfast, and with all the activity around the house lately. Those depression medications are so expensive."

"Mom, she's just a dog. I'm sure she's fine."

"Abby! You know how I feel about you calling Bailey 'just a dog.'"

"We'll go feed her right now." Abby glanced at Jade who winked at her.

"Oh good," her mom said. "I'll talk to you again soon then." She hung up the phone.

"So we're going to your house to feed your dog?" Jade asked.

"My mom's dog," Abby corrected.

Jade put his arm around her waist and pulled her close. "Sounds like fun. What's her name?"

"Her name is Bailey and she's spoiled rotten." Abby stopped, realizing that she'd come in Clarissa's car. "Can we take your car?"

"Sure." Jade gave her a little squeeze and then turned them around to head back in the other direction.

CHAPTER SEVENTEEN

ABBY HAD NEVER BROUGHT a boy home. Ben didn't really count. He came as a friend of her parents, not as her boyfriend. In fact he came over to chat with her dad more than to see her.

Abby unlocked the front door to the house, her hands clammy as she turned the door knob. Taking a deep breath she opened the door and let Jade in. He smiled as he walked past then looked up at the tall ceiling in the front entrance.

"Nice," he said.

"Thanks." Abby went to attend to Bailey right away, who was resting on the floor in a patch of sunlight. The small dog raised her little head for a moment when Jade walked by, then lowered it again and went back to her nap. She did not seem at all concerned with having missed her breakfast.

"So," Jade said, "this is your childhood home."

Abby's insides fluttered. What did he think of her home? She looked around at the perfectly clean kitchen and the adjoining large living room, trying to see it as Jade would. The house looked like a show home. It *was* a show home once and, with the help of her mother's maid, it still looked like one.

"When I see it through your eyes it does seem weird that I grew up here," Abby said. She finished changing Bailey's water then rinsed her hands in the kitchen sink. "I'll show you where I actually grew up."

Abby led Jade upstairs and down the hall to her modest sized bedroom. She opened the curtains to let in more sunlight. Her arms felt heavy, like she was too weak to use them. Having Jade in her room made her that nervous. She never brought Ben up here. When he visited, they all talked in the living room or the dining room. He'd never asked to see her bedroom and she'd never offered to show him.

Jade stepped into the room and Abby braced herself for him to make a joke about the stuffed animals or the pink wallpaper, but he didn't. The first thing he noticed was the shell necklace on her dresser.

He walked over and picked it up. "You kept it."

"Of course." Abby took the necklace from him to put it on. "I've been wearing it every day since you gave it to me. But today I didn't want to snag it on a high collared dress or something at the bridal store."

Jade stepped behind her to help fasten the clip attached to the leather chord. His fingertips brushed the back of Abby's neck, sending warm shivers down her spine. When he was done he set his hands lightly onto her shoulders and looked at her in the dresser mirror.

"You always look so beautiful," he said softly.

Abby turned to face him, and then found herself in his arms. He smelled of suntan lotion and the familiar scents of the beach. It made her long to return there again and feel the hot sun on her shoulders. Jade pulled her into a hug.

"Isn't your family going to worry about you?" she asked.

"I don't think it's possible for them to worry any more than they already do." Jade's answer seemed packed with meaning. Why were they so worried about him? She was about to ask, but then he pulled away and walked over to the computer desk. He picked up one of her drawings, the one with the character that looked like him.

"Where'd you buy this?" he asked, inspecting it. "It's really good. Looks like an original. I love Anime art." Jade looked at her. "Did you get this at a comic convention?"

"It's mine." Abby walked over to him to take the drawing.

"You drew this?" Jade's eyes widened. "This is amazing."

"It was a while ago." She took the drawing and set it into the box with the others, face down. "I don't draw anymore."

"Why not?" Jade picked out other pages from the box and looked through them. "You drew all of these?" He stopped to look more closely at a detailed drawing of two characters fighting. "Wow."

"Lots of people draw." Abby watched him inspect her artwork. Each time he touched a page it felt like he was touching her. No one but Clarissa had seen these drawings.

"Abby," Jade looked at her with intense blue eyes. "These are really good. Have you published anything yet?"

"No," She looked away. "It's just a hobby."

"Are you kidding?" Jade pulled out a few more drawings. "You could go to the Comicon in Vancouver with these. Your work is way better than a lot of the artists that go."

"I couldn't just go, I'm not famous."

"Sure you can. You just pay for a table at the artists booths."

Abby shook her head no.

"Why not?" Jade asked. "You're very talented."

Abby was too choked up to respond. Why was Jade stirring up her childhood dreams, the ones that she'd long ago given up on? She couldn't start believing in them again, not now that she was grown up and knew those types of dreams didn't come true for average people.

"Have you eaten?" Abby asked.

Jade set the pages he was holding back into the box. "I could eat," he said. "Maybe I can take you to the Comicon in Vancouver next year." He stopped, as though remembering something, then frowned. "I could definitely eat something."

CHAPTER EIGHTEEN

JADE SEEMED SUBDUED during their lunch down-stairs. The spark in his eyes was gone. Finally, after they'd cleaned up, he came out of his slump.

"Let's go line dancing tonight!" he said, spinning Abby in his arms.

She laughed. "Line dancing? Where?"

"I don't know, this is Cowboy Country isn't it? I sure passed by a lot of cows in fields on my way here."

Abby laughed again. "So you think we can just show up at some barn outside of town and we'll find cowboys wrapping up their daily chores and beginning their evening barn dance?"

"Maybe." Jade grabbed her sides to tickle her.

"Stop, I'm ticklish." She squealed and ran away. Bailey perked up and chased after them, barking at Jade.

Abby evaded Jade, determined not to get caught and be tickled further. What if he tried to kiss her? But her laughing slowed her down and Jade caught her. He pinned her against the wall near the front entrance of the house.

"Line dancing in a barn," he said, catching his breath, "happens to be on my bucket list okay?" Abby squirmed but he held onto her wrists and she couldn't get away. "Have you ever been kissed?" he asked.

When she didn't answer right away he released his grasp, placing his palms against hers and slowly slipping his fingers between hers.

"I've been kissed," Abby said, her heart racing. She clasped his fingers tightly. "But only...politely."

Jade laughed at this, his chest moving against hers. "Well then, can I kiss you politely, too?" He looked down at her lips and Abby's belly did a little flip, like she'd just dropped on a roller coaster. She didn't know how to kiss! Not in any real way at least. He was waiting for her answer.

Abby nodded, clasping his hands even tighter. He leaned forward, brushing his lips over hers. Her back arched in response and his grip on her hands tightened. He hesitated a moment then pulled back and let go of her.

Her shoulders relaxed. Just a polite kiss, that's all it was.

Jade slipped a hand behind her neck, fingers tangled in her hair, and the other behind the small of her back. A heat flowed through her, from head to toe. He was going to kiss her for real this time.

"Jade wait..." Abby set her palms against his chest, resisting his embrace. What could she say? I'm scared?

He tucked her hair behind her ear, running his thumb along her cheek, then over her bottom lip. "Can I kiss you again?" he asked, his voice husky. Their bodies moved against each other as they breathed and he waited for Abby's response. She licked her dry lips, accidentally licking Jade's thumb as well.

"I'll take that as a yes," he said, then kissed her again. This time her lips parted and their tongues touched.

Abby's toes curled and she slipped her arms around Jade's neck, pushing herself against him, wanting more.

The click of the front door being unlocked cut through their sighs.

Abby stifled a groan of disappointment as Jade separated himself from her, leaving a cold emptiness where his body had been.

The door opened and Sofia, her parents' Spanish cleaning lady, stepped in holding a bucket of supplies.

"Oh! Miss Abby!" she said, pushing her hand to her chest. "I'm sorry." She took in the sight before her. "I have forgotten that you are home now again. And you have a male company. I am sorry. I came too early."

"No, it's okay. Come in." Abby opened the door wider, helping the older lady with her vacuum. "We were just leaving."

"Thank you," Sofia nodded.

Abby let out the breath she'd been holding.

"Sofia, this is my... friend, Jade."

Jade stepped forward and offered his hand.

"Very nice to meet you," Sofia said, shaking his hand. Abby was grateful to the lady. She'd come just in time before things got too heated.

Never had Abby felt so out of control and hungry for more, rather than afraid of it. Her knees were still weak. But there was nowhere it could lead, since she couldn't have sex.

She sighed. "I need some fresh air."

CHAPTER NINETEEN

ABBY THREW HER KEYS down as she entered her apartment. They landed on the hardwood floor with a loud clatter.

"Whoops," she said. "There used to be a side table there." She removed her shoes and Jade did the same. "Well," she put her hands on her hips, surveying the room. "This is it, my old apartment." Her voice echoed in the open space.

Jade ran to the middle of the empty living room and slid across the hardwood floors in his socks, then fell onto the couch.

"I love empty apartments," he said, lying on his back and closing his eyes. Abby joined him, sitting at the opposite end by his feet. The living room was mostly empty, only the couch remained because it was too heavy for her and Clarissa to lift themselves.

"Why do you love empty apartments?" Abby asked. She loved seeing Jade so relaxed.

He put his hands behind his head and opened his eyes to meet hers. "I always wanted to move into my own apartment."

"You still live with your parents then?"

"Yeah, but not because I want to."

"They won't let you move out?"

"My mom is worried..." Jade sat up and rubbed his forehead. "I'm more tired than I thought."

Abby got up to give him room to lie down comfortably. "Of course you're tired. I'm sorry. You drove for nine hours. You should sleep for a bit."

"Where are you going?" Jade grabbed Abby around the waist with both hands and pulled her on top of him. "Rest with me."

"You need to sleep," Abby said, holding back a smile. "I've had sleep."

Jade hugged her closer. She lay her head onto his chest and settled into the couch beside him, draping one leg over his stomach.

"One sec." Jade sat up and took off his suit jacket, throwing it onto the ground. He lay back down and pulled Abby close again. She rested her hand on his white dress shirt where she could feel his heartbeat. Her nervous energy that had been with her all day began to melt away as she relaxed into his embrace. She'd just rest for a little while, then...

Then what? Then she'd tell Jade he had to go home? He'd driven all this way to spend just one more day with her. And they hadn't even spent a full day together yet. It was only about two in the afternoon.

Abby blinked at the sun shining onto them through the glass balcony doors. Its heat warmed her cheek and arm that rested on Jade. She'd never felt so comfortable in her life.

Abby's arm was cold and the apartment lay in darkness. Why was she asleep on the couch? Jade moved beneath her and she remembered, her insides fluttering.

"Hi," he said, his hand running down her back. The fluttering in her tummy sprung to life and she remembered Jade's lips on hers when they'd kissed that morning. She didn't want to move from his arms. Could he feel her heart racing against his side?

Abby's arm that she'd been laying on had fallen asleep and her bladder was full. She got up.

The street lamp outside lit the living room floor in a soft glow but the rest of the room was dark with shadows.

Jade's fingers brushed Abby's side, making their way down her arm and leaving goose bumps on her skin. He sat up too, seeming reluctant to let her go.

"We slept for a while," he said in a raspy voice.

"Yeah…" Abby got off the couch and went to switch on the light. "I'm surprised my mom didn't call a million times." She flipped the switch but the lights didn't come on. She flipped it a few more times. "There's no power?"

"Is that your phone ringing?" Jade asked. A white glow from the floor lit up the ceiling. Her phone was on silent and there was an incoming call. She picked it up off the floor. It was Ben calling.

"I'll just be a minute," she said to Jade.

"Washroom?" he asked, pointing down the hall.

Abby nodded with a thumbs up then turned her back to him, to answer the call. "Hello?"

"Hi, Abby. Is this a good time?" Ben sounded business-like, as usual. Abby stepped out of the apartment into the bright lights of the hallway.

"What's up?" she asked, closing the door behind her. Ben usually just sent texts instead of calling, unless it was important.

"Did I catch you at dinner?"

"No, I haven't had dinner yet."

"Good. I was hoping we could go for dinner and talk."

"I thought my parents were in Calgary," Abby couldn't resist saying. "Or do you mean just with me?"

"They're on their way back right now actually. But I did mean just us. How about we go to The Mix Lounge?"

Abby groaned. "They always I.D. me there, and one time someone called me your daughter, remember?" She laughed but Ben didn't. "I can't tonight anyway. Tomorrow sometime?"

"I have meetings all day tomorrow," Ben said. Abby rolled her eyes as she paced the hall, eager to get off the phone.

"Listen Abby, I know I never gave you the chance to really say yes to the engagement. I was worried you'd say no."

Abby didn't reply. It wasn't often that Ben dropped his businessman demeanour and actually said something real.

"I'm not a very emotional person," Ben continued, "so I'm not good at…expressing myself."

Abby sighed. Despite all his faults, Ben was an okay guy. He'd stuck with her for a long time and was the only long term boyfriend she'd ever really had, even if their year of dating consisted of very few actual dates.

"I just need a little time to figure things out," Abby said, looking behind her at the door.

Ben didn't respond.

"Can we talk over supper tomorrow night?" she asked.

"I have a dinner meeting tomorrow night and then—" Ben paused. "Actually, never mind. I'll cancel that. It's not that important. I'll see you tomorrow night."

"At the Mix?"

"We can go to a fast food place if you'd like."

Abby stopped pacing. This really wasn't like Ben. He hated fast food. "My favourite one downtown?"

"Sure. I'll text you." Ben was already talking to someone else before the phone call disconnected.

Abby stared at her phone for a moment. She almost preferred the emotionally distant version of Ben. This one might prove difficult to keep emotionally distant from.

A sudden chill ran through her and she hugged her arms around her body. What if Ben began to open up and want to become closer, emotionally? Physically? No, it wouldn't happen. He must want something from her and this was his way of trying to get it, by acting more vulnerable and agreeing to eat at a fast food restaurant.

With a sigh, Abby opened her apartment door and went back in. Jade was lying on the couch, the light of his cell phone shining down on him as he pressed the buttons on the screen. He glanced over at her and she smiled back.

She pointed down the hall. "I'll be right back."

In the washroom she flipped on the light switch but the lights weren't working. She took out her phone to use as a flashlight.

There were two missed calls from her mother and one text from Clarissa,

I came back to the apt. Found u and J wrapped up together like a pretzel. Not sure what's going on or if you've resolved your 'problem' ;) Call me.

Abby set the phone down and went to the washroom, then washed her hands quickly and brushed her fingers through her hair to tame the wild curls. She couldn't see her reflection in the mirror well enough to tell if she looked good or not. If only she still had some of her make-up here and a hair brush. Then again, she never wore any make-up at the beach and that's how Jade had always seen her. She grabbed her phone to reply to Clarissa's text.

Nothing's going on.

Or was there?

Back in the living room Jade was sitting on the couch, flipping his cell phone in the air and catching it again. He smiled when he saw her.

"Everything okay on your end?" she asked, sitting down beside him.

"The parents are crazy mad at me right now. But they don't know where I am exactly so they can't hunt me down."

"That's not good," Abby frowned.

"Don't worry. I told them I'm fine and that I'm going back tomorrow."

Jade's words hung in the air between them.

Abby's shoulders slumped. She looked down at the dark shadows of her hands in her lap, not sure what to say.

"So, Ben called?" Jade asked, breaking the silence.

"Yeah... You hungry?"

"Yes."

"There's a Chinese restaurant nearby."

"How about Japanese?" Jade put his arm around her.

"Japanese sounds great."

CHAPTER TWENTY

ABBY STRUGGLED TO PICK up the California Maki with her chop sticks. Jade sat in front of her in the middle of the floor. They'd picked up some candles, matches and marshmallows from a grocery store near the Japanese Restaurant on the way home.

The smell of burnt matches hung in the air, mixed with the warm scents of the pumpkin spice candles that were lit around them. Abby looked down at the guitar on the floor beside Jade. She'd seen it in the back seat of his car and brought it up.

"I'm not really any good at it you know," Jade said, nodding to the guitar. "But I suppose I'm better at it than you are at using chopsticks."

Abby stabbed her Maki down the middle and lifted it to her mouth, but it fell apart before she could close her lips around it. Jade picked up the mangled pieces from her plate with one scoop of his chopsticks and offered it to her.

"Want me to feed you?" he teased, looking down at her lips.

"I can manage," Abby said. She grabbed the Maki off of Jade's chopsticks with her fingers and shoved the whole thing into her mouth.

"You're not used to eating with chopsticks?" Jade asked.

"No," Abby said, her cheeks flushing. "We only eat Japanese food once a year, on Christmas Day."

"On Christmas Day? No Turkey with all the trimmings?"

"My mom hosts a big Christmas party every year, with Turkey and all that, in the beginning of December. On Christmas Day everyone is with their own families so it's just me and my mom and dad. It's the only time I ever see my mom in sweatpants and a t-shirt."

Abby looked at Jade to see if he was bored, but he seemed interested so she continued. "All the stores are closed on Christmas Day so we stay at home, watch

Rudolf and eat reheated Japanese food from the day before."

Jade smiled, then ate another Maki. Abby waited for him to say something about his family Christmases, but he didn't. He never said much about his family or himself it seemed.

He poked around in the take out containers with his chopsticks, his eyes catching the candlelight, his hair curling up at the ends. He was like a Christmas present, one she'd always wanted but never thought she'd get.

"What are you thinking about?" Jade asked, looking up and catching her staring.

"Thinking about?" Abby scooted away from him, knocking over a candle that was behind her. He quickly grabbed for it, leaning forward and catching it just in time, then setting it straight again. His shoulder brushed hers and she stiffened. He pulled back, giving her some room, but staying close.

"Come with me," he said, reaching up to touch her cheek.

Abby held her breath. He was so close.

She wanted him to kiss her again, even if all the strong emotions it awakened scared her. But he didn't kiss her. He was waiting for her to answer.

"Go with you? Where would we go?" Abby said, pulling away from his touch to clear her head.

"You're right." Jade sat back and picked up the candle nearest him, inspecting the flame. "I still live with my parents."

"And I still live with mine." Abby sighed. "Don't you just wish you could get away from them? Be totally free, as though they didn't even exist?"

"Yes." Jade set down the candle. His shoulders slumped. "But it's not that simple. They do exist and I can't just ignore them."

Abby nodded. "I know exactly what you mean."

"Do your parents worry about you too?"

"Yes, but it's not just that. I don't know if I'd get too far without them and I think they know that." Abby's cheeks heated up. She didn't want Jade to know how dependent she was, and yet he seemed to understand.

"I wouldn't either actually," he said. "Not for long anyway."

"What do you mean?" Abby studied Jade's face, hoping to get a clue as to what he meant. Was something holding him back from being on his own? For her it was her fears and anxieties more than anything, but Jade didn't seem the type of person that would have such issues.

"Want me to play you a song?" he asked, picking up his guitar.

"Okay," Abby smiled. She could tell he didn't want to open up, and she wouldn't push him. He took out the guitar pick that was set between the strings at the guitar neck and strummed a chord. "I always wanted to be in a band," he said as he tuned the guitar.

"Maybe you will be one day." Abby clasped her hands together and prepared to listen to his song.

"I won't. There's not enough time for stuff like that."

"For what? Being in a band?"

He ignored her question and strummed another note, then another, humming along and changing the chord until he was satisfied.

"*Let's write our song together,*" Jade began. His singing voice had a rough and breathy sound to it. Abby closed her eyes and listened.

"*And send secret letters, in another world that will last forever, where we have more than just this moment. Because there's nothing I can do.*" Jade stopped, clearing his voice and changing the chord again.

"*I've already lost, and you'll just get hurt, there's nothing I can do, I know this can't work. But there might just be something real, here, between me and you, something true, but we'll never know, because there's nothing I can do, nothing I can do, to stay here, beside you, nothing I can do, to give you, all you deserve, as I should, as I wish I could, There's only a moment, only this moment I have with you.*"

He strummed the last note and the apartment lay in silence. Abby opened her eyes, finding it hard to swallow. She wasn't sure if he'd written the song for her but it made her sad. He set down his guitar and bowed his head. Her heart clenched.

This whole time that she'd been trying to figure out how she felt, about Ben and Jade, and her future. Yet she'd never considered how Jade felt.

He looked up at her, his eyes full of emotion. "I've made you sad," he said, getting up. "If this is my last night with you then let's do something fun and not be sad."

Abby got up too. "Like what? It's getting late."

"When's the last time you stayed up all night?"

"Willingly?" Abby thought for a moment. "I think never."

Jade laughed. "I'm not about to sleep away my last night with you. Let's start by roasting those marshmallows."

Jade went to the counter to grab the bag of marshmallows and Abby jumped up to get to them first. She swiped them out of his hands and he tackled her onto the couch.

"Hey, you'll squish the marshmallows," she said.

"Sorry." He got up and offered his hand to help her up. She took it, secretly wishing he'd continued wrestling with her on the couch.

He snatched the bag away from her.

"Hey!" Abby yelled, chasing after him.

* * *

"I think I'm just charring the outside," Abby said, inspecting the brown and black spotted marshmallow at the end of her chopstick. "It hasn't puffed up at all."

Jade set his own marshmallow down on the lid of a take-out container. "Let me see." He took Abby's marshmallow off of her stick with his fingers.

"Hey, that's mine!" Abby grabbed for it but Jade quickly bit it in half.

"See it's soft in the middle," he said, showing her the sticky marshmallow. He offered her the other half.

Abby took a hold of his hand to steady it, then ate the rest of the marshmallow from his fingertips, not wanting to dirty her own hands. She wrapped her lips around his finger, trying to get a sticky part off.

"Abby...stop." Jade moved his hand away and quickly got up.

"What wrong?" Abby asked, but Jade had already disappeared into the darkness that lay outside of the candlelight. "I'll just wash my hands," she heard him say, followed by the sound of the water running in the sink.

She took another marshmallow from the bag and stuck it onto the end of her chopstick, deciding to roast another one. The half marshmallow she'd eaten from Jade's fingers had tasted really good and she wanted another one.

"Hypothetical question," Jade said, returning to their candlelit area. His shirt sleeves were rolled up to the elbows and the top buttons of his dress shirt were now undone.

He sat down beside Abby. "Would you still marry Ben, if you only had one year left to live?"

"No," Abby said without hesitation.

"You didn't take a lot of time to think about that," Jade said, watching her.

"If I just had a year left I'd spend the time with my parents and Clarissa...and you."

Jade nodded, thinking. His hair was disheveled and hung into his eyes.

"Have you ever made a bucket list?" he asked after a moment.

"No. Have you?"

"I've got one in my head."

Abby abandoned her marshmallow and pulled out her cell phone. "I'm going to write one now."

Jade took out his cell phone too. "Text your list to me and I'll text you mine," he said, laying back onto the hardwood floor. He held his phone up in front of him and began typing away.

Abby pulled her legs up to her chest and set her phone onto her knees, close to her face, like she was typing a secret message.

She had to think for a moment. She'd never put any thought into a bucket list before. Jade, on the other hand, didn't seem to need any time to think over his.

Less than a minute later Abby's notification bar showed a new text message from Jade.

She looked over at him. "Give me a minute, I'm still thinking."

"No rush." He winked at her, then went back to his phone.

Abby thought about what she'd want to do before she died. She'd always wanted a dog, not a small one like her mom's dog but a big one that would roam on a farm. She lived in a province with lots of farmers but had never been on a farm herself. Living on one wouldn't be on her bucket list though. She wasn't sturdy enough to be a farm girl. Then there was the whole marriage and family thing that she had to start getting around to doing soon.

Finally, after some thought, Abby came up with the following list:

-Go to Disneyland

-Have sex (maybe)

-Get a dog

-Get a tattoo

-Have a Baby

-Become financially independent

-Publish my comic books

-Go to a Rock Concert

-Visit Grandparents in Ontario one day

-Go to Hawaii

-Hear the Four Seasons live at the Symphony

She sent the list to Jade and his phone vibrated. He opened the text and laughed.

"Are you planning to do these things in this order?"

"No." Abby gave Jade a look then opened his text.

-Go line dancing

-Crash my car

-Have a baby

-Climb a mountain

-Fall in love

-Go bungee jumping

-Get drunk

-Get a tattoo

-Watch LOTR *and The Hobbit*

-Go Caroling

-Go caving

-Join the SETI League

"Interesting list," Abby chuckled. "What's SETI?"

"Searching for Extra-terrestrial Intelligence."

Abby laughed. "Nice. Well I might add *get drunk* to my list too I think," she said.

"You've never been drunk?"

"No. I've never drank before. Well, other than sips of wine."

Jade sat up and looked at her.

"Are you religious?"

"No, just scared to drink or get drunk. Knowing my luck I'd have an allergic reaction and die."

"But you're not scared anymore?" His eyes searched hers.

"I don't know, maybe. I'll just get drunk when I'm 80, then if I die at least I'll have lived most of my life already. What about you? You've never drank?"

"My dad's a pastor," Jade said, looking at his cell phone again. "Hey, we both have *get a tattoo* on our lists."

"And *have a baby*," Abby added. "But I don't see how you can have one Jade, since you're a guy."

"You know what I mean," he smiled, still looking at his phone. "You have *publish my comic books*."

"I'm waiting until I'm almost dead for that too. Then I'll publish them and my chances of being famous will increase with my death, because people will feel they owe it to me as a tribute to my life to buy them." Abby giggled but Jade simply ignored the comment.

"You've never been to a rock concert?" he asked.

"Nope."

"My favourite rock band is doing a concert in

Vancouver in September. Do you want me to take you?"

"Isn't Vancouver a little far?"

"I live there."

Abby nodded, looking at Jade's list again. "You don't have a lot of crazy things on your list," she said. "Like bridge jumping or cliff diving. Or even going to Hawaii or Australia."

"Travelling is too time consuming. Don't you already have a dog?"

"That's my Mom's dog. And it's small. I want to have a big, slobbery dog that knocks over wine glasses left on coffee tables and bangs into people and eats slippers for breakfast."

Jade laughed. "Okay I'm adding *big, slobbery dog* to my bucket list then too."

Abby watched him paste his old list into a new message and add *big slobbery dog* to it.

"Here's the updated version," he said. "Oh and I have something on my list that I can take off now cuz I've already done it."

"I hope it's line dancing, because I'm not going, sorry."

Abby's phone vibrated with Jade's new list. She scrolled between the two messages to see what he'd taken off, but an incoming text from Clarissa interrupted her.

Are you okay?

Abby texted back right away,

Yes I'm fine :)

A few seconds later she got a reply.

What are you doing? Are you busy?

Abby stared at the text for a moment, not sure how to respond. She didn't want to be one of those girls that forgot about her best friend when a guy came along. But Clarissa had been disappointed to see Jade at the bridal shop earlier so she'd be even more disappointed to find out Abby was with him right now.

"Do you have a black pen?" Jade asked, pulling her out of her thoughts.

"In my purse." She set her phone down, deciding not to answer Clarissa's text for now.

"Can you draw your anime character on my back? Like a tattoo?" Jade asked, starting to unbutton his shirt.

Abby's pulse sped up. She shrugged in response, pulling her knees up to her chest again and hugging them tight.

"Please?" Jade moved in closer.

"Why?" Abby's cheeks grew warm as he undid a few more buttons.

"It's the closest thing I'm ever going to get to a real tattoo."

"You can get a real one can't you?"

Jade stopped unbuttoning his shirt and got up.

"Yeah, I guess," he said.

He began clearing away their food containers and gathering them all into the large paper bag they'd come in.

"It would just wash off anyway," Abby said, feeling guilty that she was too shy to do something like draw on a guy's back.

"Don't worry about it," Jade said, giving her a quick smile then continuing with his cleaning.

Abby stood up and got her purse from the front entrance. There was a pen in there somewhere.

"Jade?" She put her hand on his arm to stop him from cleaning. "Which character do you want me to draw?"

CHAPTER TWENTY-ONE

GATHERING THE CANDLES AROUND them for better light, Abby knelt down behind Jade.

He slid his shirt off and threw it onto the couch. Her fingers hovered over his back. She wouldn't be able to draw without resting her palm on his bare skin, but the idea seemed so intimate. Too intimate.

The room was much too warm from the candles. Abby got up and went to open the balcony doors to let in the night air. It wasn't much cooler outside than inside, but at least there was some air movement now.

The candles flickered in the slight breeze. Abby returned to her spot where Jade waited patiently. She let out the breath she'd been holding and set her left hand onto his shoulder to steady herself. His skin was warm and his muscles relaxed beneath her touch.

She ran her fingers over his back, studying her canvas as she planned out her drawing. "How big do you want it?"

"Whatever takes the longest time to draw," Jade said.

Abby smiled. "I'm just going to do something basic."

"We've got all night." He turned to look at her over his shoulder.

"Don't move," Abby said, turning him back.

Then she began to draw.

She'd keep the drawing small and just on his right shoulder.

Soon she was lost in her work, adding details and retreating into her own world.

When she was finally done she sat back to admire her work. It was fantastic.

"Too bad it's not permanent," she said to herself.

Jade turned to face her and suddenly he was only inches from her. The pen dropped from her hand.

It was the middle of the night and Jade was shirtless, by candlelight, looking down at her lips.

"It's your turn," he whispered. His breath tickled her cheek. He picked up the pen and sat back.

"Me?" Abby blinked.

"Yes, you." Jade said. "You have, *get a tattoo,* on your bucket list too, don't you?"

"Yes, but a real tattoo, not a pen version."

Jade gave her playful grin. "Don't you want to see how it looks on you first, before you get a real one?"

Abby nodded. "I guess."

"What would you get, if you got a real tattoo?"

"Three birds, ravens, like in a movie I saw once."

"Good choice." Jade grabbed his phone and searched for an image online. Abby got into a cross-legged position, her heart settling down a bit as she waited.

"Like this?" Jade held the phone out for her to see. The picture was of a girl with three black ravens tattooed onto her chest, near the collar bone at her right shoulder. Abby's hand went up to the collar of her blouse. He'd be drawing on her there?

Jade set his phone down on the floor beside her, with the image displayed. "I think I can draw it." Sliding towards her, he moved as close as he could, until their knees touched.

"Do you want it in the same place as she has it?" He asked, reaching up and touching her neck. His touch sent a trail of electricity down Abby's back.

"Here?" Jade moved the collar of her blouse to the side and her head tilted in the opposite direction, allowing him more access to her neck.

"I think it's lower," she whispered, her pulse racing beneath his fingertips. With unsteady fingers she unbuttoned the top of her blouse. Jade slid his hand beneath the light fabric, sliding it off her shoulder. He started to move her bra strap down then stopped. Their eyes met.

There was a question in his eyes as he waited for her permission. Abby answered with a smile. He slid the bra strap the rest of the way off her shoulder and she closed her eyes. Her chest rose as she took in a slow breath, meeting his warm palm. He rested his hand down and she felt the tip of the ink pen begin to glide over her skin as he drew. It rolled in cool, smooth strokes.

"Two," Abby whispered.

"Two?" Jade asked, his voice thick with emotion.

"Yes. Just two birds, please."

"Okay." He continued drawing. Each pen stroke, each movement of his fingers, sent shivers through Abby. What would his lips feel like caressing the same places that the pen traveled along her skin?

Jade's breath tickled her neck as he worked in silent concentration.

Then suddenly he moved away. "All done," he said, setting her blouse back onto her shoulder. The unbuttoned front fell forward, opening up and exposing her bra. His eyes trailed down and then back up again to meet hers.

He leaned towards her, his hand reaching up behind her head, fingers tangling in her hair. Abby moved closer, eager for his kiss.

The click of the front door lock echoed through the room and they jumped apart. Abby quickly buttoned her shirt and stood up to go to the door. Jade grabbed his own shirt off the couch and put it on.

Only one person had the key to this apartment and it was Clarissa. Abby sighed in frustration. The girl had the worst timing.

CHAPTER TWENTY-TWO

"ABBY?" CLARISSA WHISPERED, squinting her eyes as though searching for Abby in the dark. The bright hallway lights silhouetted her frame in the doorway. She flicked the light switch on and off.

"The electricity isn't working," Abby rushed over to the door. She cleared her throat, which sounded husky and unlike her.

"Oh, you're awake." Clarissa stopped fiddling with the light switch and looked down at Abby's blouse. "Abby Elizabeth Blosym! Is your shirt buttoned up the wrong way?" Her eyes scanned the dark apartment again.

Abby pushed her out of the room and into the hallway before she said anything more embarrassing.

"I didn't realize I'd be interrupting something," Clarissa said wide eyed.

"You weren't." Abby's cheeks grew hot. She pushed the door closed behind her.

"That's not what it looks like to me."

"Clarissa, is there a reason you came by?"

"Yes, sorry. But I didn't think you'd actually be awake and, um, unbuttoned."

"Why are you up at 4am?" Abby sighed, crossing her arms. She was trying to be serious but a grin crept up on her.

"It's 5 am actually. I guess time flies when you're having fun?" Clarissa winked. "I can come back later after I get some sleep, we were just in the neighbourhood and I wanted to pick up my—"

"What's this?" Abby grabbed Clarissa's hand to inspect the diamond ring on her ring finger. "You're—"

"Engaged!" Clarissa gushed. "Matt proposed tonight, or technically last night I guess. I was going to tell you but I didn't want to do it over text. Not that you were even answering your texts."

"I'm so happy for you!" Abby hugged her friend. "So you really love him then? This is the real deal?"

"Yes." Clarissa squeezed Abby then let her go. "If wanting to settle down and spend the rest of your life with one special person is considered love then yes, I definitely love him. He can be a little jealous but that's only because he loves me too much."

"Congratulations!" Abby said, getting teary-eyed. "Really, I mean it. I'm so happy for you."

"I'm happy for you too. I've never seen you so..." Clarissa looked at her for a moment. "So free, like you're finally coming out of your shell."

Abby shrugged, not sure how to respond to that.

"Are we in some kind of alternate universe?" Clarissa asked. "Me, engaged to be married and settling down. You, making out with a guy in the middle of the night, while engaged to a rich man."

"Oh, no." Abby covered her face with her hands. "When you put it that way..."

"What? No." Clarissa pulled Abby's hands away from her face. "I'm not judging you. Sorry, that came out wrong. It just seems like our roles are a little reversed now, that's all."

"Now you're really scaring me," Abby said, but she smiled. "Don't start having any babies and becoming a soccer mom just yet, okay? Give me a little time to catch up."

"You don't need to worry about that," Clarissa said. "I won't be ready to change diapers for a while yet."

"Okay, good." Abby adjusted the buttons of her blouse so they were buttoned up the right way. "I'd better get back to Jade."

Clarissa laughed. "Okay, you do that. And don't do anything I wouldn't do."

Abby rolled her eyes, then slipped quietly back into the room, giving Clarissa a little wave before closing the door behind her.

CHAPTER TWENTY-THREE

THE LIGHT OF DAWN spread over the apartment and Abby could see Jade lying on the couch, phone in hand, eyes closed. She walked over to him but he didn't open his eyes. He was breathing slowly. A curl of dark hair lay on his cheek, accentuating his strong jaw line.

Abby knelt down, reaching out to brush the curl aside but then stopped. He was asleep. Should she wake him? He'd want her to. They were supposed to stay up all night together. But he looked so peaceful. She didn't have the heart to wake him. He'd driven all night to get here.

She walked over to the patio doors and closed the blinds, shutting out the oncoming daylight. But the blinds couldn't shut out the harsh realities of the day.

The candlelit darkness of their night spent together was gone now. Abby wanted the night to last forever, for Jade to kiss her and never stop. But he was leaving today. The thought was sobering, making her feel sick.

There really were no options. Jade would return to B.C. to finish his summer vacation with his family and she would marry Ben. If she didn't, her dad would lose his business. He'd worked so hard for his company, starting with nothing and making it a success.

Ben would help them keep the business in the family. It wasn't about the money, even if her parents would be okay living off her mother's cleaning business. Her dad didn't deserve to lose everything. She couldn't imagine running off with Jade anyway and leaving her parents behind to worry.

Marrying Ben was what was best for her. It was best for Jade too. He was young and still had college to go through, parties to attend with his friends and all the stuff young guys do. Abby didn't fit into that picture.

She sat down on the floor, not sure where to go at the moment. She was too awake with all the thoughts running through her head to get any sleep. She checked her phone. No calls or messages from her mom, which was surprising. Remembering Jade's bucket list, she opened it and compared the two lists he'd sent.

> *Crash my car*
> *Have a baby*
> *Climb a mountain*
> *Fall in love...*

There it was, the item that was removed from the second list, *fall in love*. Abby scrolled up and down again just to be sure. Yes, that was what he'd taken off his new list. Her chest tightened. He loved her?

She got up, pulse racing. Ben didn't love her, even after dating for so long. A little flame lit inside of her and was quickly growing. Jade had asked her to go with him. She would go.

Abby texted a quick note to his phone then left the apartment.

CHAPTER TWENTY-FOUR

EVERYONE WAS ALREADY AWAKE when Abby arrived at home an hour later. She'd waited for the bus, done a transfer, then walked a few more blocks before finally getting home.

Her mom was in the living room, looking through bills, and her dad was in the kitchen. Abby walked by them as quietly as she could.

"Where are you coming from?" her mom asked, not looking up from the papers in her hand. "I thought you were upstairs asleep."

"Oh, I went for an early morning jog," Abby said. It wasn't entirely a lie. She *had* jogged part of the way home.

Her dad lowered his newspaper and gave her a questioning look. He always knew when she was lying.

Why couldn't she just be straight forward with her mother? *I spent the night at the apartment with a guy I'm falling in love with and I've decided to follow him to B.C. Oh and by the way, you'd totally disapprove of him. He isn't rich.*

"I'm going upstairs to pack. I mean to shower," Abby said. She could feel her dad's eyes on her back as she ran up the stairs.

In her room, the box of drawings was still open and the page Jade had been looking at sat on her bed. She picked up the drawing and smiled. He believed in her and her dreams. He thought her work was good enough to take to a convention. Maybe she could publish her work someday.

She grabbed one of her completed comic book samples, original drawings with the pages stapled together into a small book, and set it onto her bed to pack with her stuff. She'd show it to Jade. It was a sample of her best work.

Not wanting to take more than one large suitcase, Abby packed for warm weather. She wouldn't worry about anything beyond that for now. Her bathroom stuff was still packed in a carrying case from the recent trip with Clarissa. She grabbed a pillow off the bed and Oggy too. Now all she needed was a sleeping bag from the basement. And maybe a quick shower.

An hour later, after her shower, Abby was bringing a sleeping bag up from the basement when her cell phone rang. She scrambled to get it, stopping halfway up the stairs. The call display said Jade.

"Hello?" she answered.

"Abby? Where are you?" He sounded worried. "Why did you leave? Why did you let me sleep?"

"I'm sorry. I didn't want to wake you because you were up all night and..." Abby felt silly. She shouldn't have snuck off like that. "Sorry. I sent you a text."

"That's okay," Jade said with a sigh. "I just really wanted to watch the sunrise with you."

"I came home to pa—."

"Can I come see you?"

Abby smiled. It would be much better to tell him in person that she'd decided to go with him.

"Yes. I'm at home." The memory of their candle-lit evening flashed through her thoughts. Jade's palm sliding over her chest as he drew the ravens. Her fingers on his bare back as she studied the most enticing canvas she'd ever drawn on.

"Abby? Are you still there?"

"Yes."

"What's your address again?"

Abby gave him the address and they got off the phone. She ran up the stairs with the sleeping bag. Her dad was still in the kitchen looking at the newspaper.

"Where's mom?"

"She went to see the accountant," he said, removing his reading glasses and looking at the sleeping bag in Abby's hand. "You're leaving?"

"Yes." A lump formed in Abby's throat. She was falling in love with Jade, but she loved her father too. What could she say to her dad? Where *was* she going exactly? To be with Jade forever? Just for a vacation until the end of summer?

Not sure what to say, she simply said, "tell mom to call me later." Then she gave her dad a hug and left.

CHAPTER TWENTY-FIVE

ABBY SAT ON HER SUITCASE, her foot tapping the pavement as she waited. A moment later Jade's car came speeding down the road. She jumped up and waved.

Jade got out of his car almost before it even came to a stop. He ran to Abby and embraced her.

"Why did you leave?" he asked, hugging her tight. "I wanted to spend every second with you while I was here."

"I thought you could use some sleep."

"I hate sleep, a whole eight hours, gone just like that." He set her down and stepped back, his hands clasping her waist. The heat from his palms warmed her skin through her shirt. "Why do you have your suit-case?"

"I'm going to come with you!" Abby said, hugging him.

"What?" Jade pulled back. He looked concerned.

"You asked me to come with you, remember?" Abby said, her smile fading. "Last night..."

Jade took his hands off her waist, leaving her sides feeling cold.

"Yes, but you were right," he said. "Where would you stay?"

Abby's heart squeezed tight. Was he serious?

"You have no future with me, trust me," Jade continued, closing his eyes for a second. "Your life is here. It's better if you stay here."

She wanted to argue but no words came.

Jade frowned. "I do want to spend time with you. You have no idea how much. I'd spend the rest of my life with you if I could." He kicked at a rock on the road, sending it flying into the grass.

"Then I don't understand," Abby said.

"It wouldn't be fair to you."

"Why is everyone telling me what they think is best for me?" Abby yelled. "What about what *I think* is best for me?"

"Maybe you don't know what that is," Jade said softly.

"What?" She couldn't believe what she was hearing. "You sound like my mother, you know."

Jade bowed his head and Abby stopped. She hated arguing with him like this. All she wanted was to have his arms around her again and to tell him she loved him. But instead she was yelling at him.

"You have no idea how much I just want things to be uncomplicated," Jade looked up. "I'd love to just have fun with you and pretend that nothing else matters." His voice rose.

Abby clenched her fists tight, fighting back tears. "You asked me, if I had one year to live, would I spend it with Ben." Her voice trembled but she continued. "Well, I'd spend it with you."

"That's just it Abby." Jade grabbed her by the upper arms and she stiffened in surprise. "Don't you get it? That was just a hypothetical situation. You don't have just one year, you have lots and lots of years. And Ben can be there for you for all of those years."

Abby pulled away from his grasp. Was he really telling her to stay with Ben? She'd almost given so much up for him and he wasn't even going to try and make it work.

"I don't love Ben," she said quietly. She wanted to yell it, but her eyes were already full of tears and there would be a flood of them if she showed any more emotion.

"Abby, please don't." Jade rubbed at his eyes, taking a deep breath. "I have to be with my parents right now. There's something I haven't told you. I'm... I'm..." He shook his head but couldn't seem to say anything.

"You're what?" Abby asked.

He took a moment longer then finally said, "I'm worried about my mom, she's sick and... and it's all very depressing. You deserve to be happy and not worry about those kind of things."

Suddenly Abby felt selfish.

"I'm sorry," Jade continued, avoiding her eyes.

Abby's shoulders slumped. This wasn't the right time for him to start a relationship. And even if it was it didn't make sense for them to be together. He was too young. She was just kidding herself. "So this is goodbye then?"

Jade nodded, backing away.

He didn't hug her, or kiss her, or touch her hand. He walked to his car door and opened it. He hesitated before getting in.

"Abby?" he said, looking at her finally.

"Yes?"

"I lo…" he stopped. "Can I please have one of your drawings to take with me?"

Kicking her suitcase over, the tears finally flowing, Abby unzipped it and took out her booklet she'd packed. She grasped it tight then threw it as hard as she could across the car hood at Jade. He caught it before it hit him in the face.

"Take it. I don't need it." Abby said. *And I don't need you*, she thought, but didn't say it.

Jade looked hurt but didn't reply.

Abandoning the suitcase, Abby ran back into the house and straight into her dad's arms, crying like she hadn't done since she was seven.

If he was surprised, he didn't show it.

"Daddy, I don't want to marry Ben," she cried. "But I don't want you to lose your company and I know marrying Ben is the right thing to do but—"

"What are you talking about?" her dad said. Abby wiped at her tears. Her breath came out in short sobs and she was having a hard time talking.

"If... if I don't marry Ben, then... then you'll lose the company," she managed to say.

"Who told you that?" Her dad looked upset.

"Ben."

He shook his head. "I don't know what will happen with the company, but it has nothing to do with you, okay?"

"But—"

"Do you love Ben?"

Abby shook her head.

"Then we'll figure it out some other way." Her dad pulled her back into a hug and this time Abby didn't cry.

She was free.

CHAPTER TWENTY-SIX

"OKAY, THEN WE'RE AGREED," Abby's mother stated matter-of-factly. "For the centerpieces we'll have the colourful Peruvian Lily arrangement. For the bouquet we'll have the traditional 'hint of snow' rose bouquet with baby's breath. For the bridesmaids bouquets we'll have the Heavenly Glee Bouquet. And lastly, rose petals on the tables." She set a handful of pamphlets onto the coffee table, adding them to the pile she'd collected over the last few days.

Abby hadn't said anything to her mom yet about cancelling the wedding, in fact, she hadn't said a word all afternoon, not since Jade left that morning. She felt like a zombie, with a bad cold. Her mom hadn't even noticed.

"I want the woven dream wedding bouquet with the light pink roses in the middle," Abby said, just to be contradictory. Even with her emotional numbness from losing Jade she could still feel the familiar defeat of having her mother chose everything for her. She hated it.

In a way, that was one of the special things about finding Jade. He'd been *her* choice, not her mother's or anyone else's. She'd found him and fallen in love with him. Ben was her mother's acquaintance through a friend. She couldn't believe she'd almost agreed to marry him.

"Pink?" Abby's mother looked at her over the top of her reading glasses. "Wouldn't it be so much lovelier all white?"

"There's white in it." Abby held up the brochure with the picture of the woven dream bouquet on it. "The pink roses are surrounded by white ones."

A rustling of a newspaper from the kitchen reminded her that her dad was within earshot. She never contradicted her mother like this, learning long ago that there was no point. But today was going to be different.

"Yes," her mother said, sounding disappointed. "It's surrounded by white, but the pink in the middle stains it."

"Exactly." Abby gave her a wry smile. "A stained bouquet for a stained, imperfect wedding."

Her mom ignored the comment and returned to the pamphlets. "We'll have to put in the order soon, so they arrive on time for the wedding."

"Oh. When's my wedding anyway?" Abby asked with mock cheerfulness. "No one's told me yet."

"We had to schedule it for the middle of October. It was the only date we could book for the United Church."

"So I'm United now?"

Her mother removed her glasses. "Don't be smart, Abby," she said. "I don't like your tone of voice."

"Look at my face mom!" Abby yelled, getting up. "Look at me. You never look at me!"

"What are you talking about?" Her mother's eyebrows shot up in surprise. "What is going on with you today?"

"You have no idea what's going on, and do you know why? Because I don't tell you. I don't want you to know. And I don't want your opinions or to be told what to do all the time. I'm a grown woman. You know that, right?"

Her mom looked offended. "Calm down. Of course I know that! You're getting married aren't you? I'm just trying to help you out because I'm your mother."

"Then help me by letting me go."

"I am letting you go. You're getting married."

"You want me to marry Ben so that you can keep running my life for me."

"That's ridiculous," her mom waved her hand at Abby, as though dismissing the idea. "You're just having a bit of wedding jitters."

"It's not wedding jitters."

"I had them too, with your father." She was no longer listening.

Abby's dad looked up from his newspaper but didn't say anything. For some reason, this made Abby angry. Why did he never get involved or stick up for her?

He knew she didn't love Ben and wouldn't be marrying him. Why hadn't he told her mother?

Abby pushed down her anger, as she always did, not wanting to get upset at her parents. Except this time she wasn't going to back down.

"I'm not marrying Ben," she said calmly, exchanging glances with her dad for a moment. She half expected him to get up and leave until the storm blew over.

Her mom began cleaning up the pamphlets, still not looking at Abby. "There's lots of time to prepare for the wedding. You don't need to worry."

"I'm in love with someone else," Abby said.

Her mother sighed dramatically. "If this is about the woven dream bouquet then we'll order that one."

"It's not about the woven dream bouquet!" Abby yelled, snatching a handful of pamphlets from the coffee table and tossing them onto the floor.

"Abby!" The anger in her mother's voice made Abby jump.

"I'm sorry, mom," she said quickly, scrambling to pick up the pamphlets.

Her mom smoothed back her hair and adjusted her skirt. "We'll talk about the flowers later, when you're not so tired." She stood up to leave.

Abby set the pamphlets back onto the table and stood up straight. "I'm not going to marry Ben, because I don't love him," she said, more quietly this time. She didn't want to get into a yelling match with her mom, it scared her. But she wasn't going to agree to marry Ben just because her mother was intimidating her.

Her mom rubbed her forehead. "I have a headache."

"I'm sorry you have a headache, but I'm not marrying Ben," Abby repeated.

"Abby, please stop. Why are you acting like this? Your father and I love you and we want what's best for you."

"I know," Abby sighed. Usually her mom's guilt trips would make her mad at herself for upsetting the family. But today she didn't see a hurt and upset mom, she only saw a manipulative one.

"I need to go," she said.

Then she walked out of the room, leaving her mom in a stunned silence.

CHAPTER TWENTY-SEVEN

"**A**BBY, SERIOUSLY, EAT SOMETHING. If this is some kind of wedding dress diet I'm going to kill you," Clarissa said.

They were at Abby's favourite fast food place, but today the smell of the chicken was making her stomach turn. She'd asked Clarissa to join her for lunch so she could tell her about the cancelled wedding and all that happened with Jade, but now she felt too depressed to talk about any of it.

"You don't have to tell me what happened if you don't want to," Clarissa said softly, picking at her food.

"I flipped out at my mom." Abby swallowed hard, blinking back tears.

"Oh…" Clarissa set her hand over Abby's. The simple touch caused a flood of tears to fall. The cashier glanced at them from behind the front counter, then left to go to the back. There were no other customers in the small fast-food restaurant, which was really just a drive thru location but had two tables inside with chairs.

"Even if marrying Ben is the logical thing to do, I don't love him. I think I'm in love with Jade." Abby stopped to wipe her eyes with a napkin.

"Are you sure?" Clarissa asked, a worried expression on her face.

"His touches are like drinking water when you're really thirsty. When I'm with him everything is okay. I stop feeling shaky." Abby held out her hand for Clarissa to see. It trembled slightly. "See."

"You need to eat."

"I need to sleep too, but I can't do that either. I know if Jade was beside me I'd fall asleep instantly."

"This is all kind of sudden isn't it?"

"I know..." Abby's shoulders slumped. "What's wrong with me?"

"You're just love sick," Clarissa said, rubbing Abby's back.

"But *you've* never been like this before."

"I know, but you're so intense."

"Maybe that's why I can't have sex, because it would just be too intense for me or something, and my body is rejecting it for my own good."

"So you didn't have sex with Jade?"

"Of course not! Look how upset I am already." Abby sniffled. "And all we did was kiss."

"He kissed you?" Clarissa smiled. "Like a real kiss, right?"

Abby smiled. "Yes!" She clapped her hands together. "Oh Clarissa, it was like fire and water at the same time."

Clarissa simply nodded, but looked confused.

"It's like he opened up a new side of me that I never knew existed," Abby continued. "My life was on pause, suspended until the moment he kissed me. And when we kiss it's like I want to kiss forever and never stop, or at least until I fall asleep in his arms. Everything else seems like a waste of time, an interruption to being together."

"Wow," Clarissa put down the piece of chicken she was about to eat. "That sounds more intense than any sexual experience I've ever had. I've never been love sick or weak at the knees, feeling faint, or any of that good stuff."

Abby nodded. Clarissa was a strong person who enjoyed intimacy but didn't get overwhelmed by it. It was nice to be able to talk to her, even if they were so different.

"The first time I had sex," Clarissa continued, "was in the back seat of this guy's car. He was two years older than me and smelled like beer. It didn't feel that great and I didn't enjoy it cuz it was my first time, but then it got easier. Even my best experiences are still just...not as intense as what you're describing."

"But being love sick is kind of unhealthy isn't it? I swear by this time next year I'll be shriveled to nothing," Abby said.

Clarissa laughed. "Oh, Abby, you're so dramatic. It will pass."

"It will never pass." Abby shook her head. "I can never un-love Jade."

"Then don't try to," Clarissa shrugged, sipping her soda. "Go with him."

Abby shook her head. "I can't. He left and said he doesn't want me to go."

"No, what you told me was that he said he needs to be with his mom right now, and it wouldn't be fair to you if he dragged you along. Can you imagine how guilty he feels if his mother only has like two months left to live or something?"

"I can't even imagine."

"When a guy tells me that it's best I'm not with him for *my* sake I just say, what's best for me is to be with you!"

Abby shook her head. "I tried that."

"Then a month later we end up breaking up anyway," Clarissa shrugged.

Abby laughed.

"Tell him you understand there's no future for you two right now," Clarissa continued. "Like marriage, a house and a baby, and all that, but that it's okay with you. All you want is to be there for him right now, even if it's *not fair to you*. See what he says."

"But it isn't fair to him. I can't interfere in his life right now, when his mom is sick."

"Maybe he could really use someone to cheer him up and be there for him. I bet he's more concerned about your future and all that, than he is about himself."

Abby felt torn. Would it be a bad idea to try and follow Jade?

"All his reasons were because he didn't think it would be fair to me," she said, thinking back to what he'd said. "But I'll tell him I'm not worried about marriage and kids and all that right now, and that I just want to be there for him, even if it's only for a few weeks until the end of summer. Then whatever happens after that, happens. I've got nothing to lose by asking."

Clarissa smiled. "That's the spirit! What guy could argue with that, right?"

"But doesn't that seem irresponsible?" Abby asked.

"No, it's living in the moment, and that's totally okay."

Abby sat back. She'd stopped shaking and her stomach had unclenched completely at the thought of following her heart. She wasn't sure what would happen but she had to try. And if Jade didn't want her to go with him, even after she explained how she felt, then at least she would know that she'd tried.

"I'm so ready to eat now," she said, taking out some chicken from the small bucket they'd ordered. It was cold but she didn't care, she was starving. "Thanks, Clarissa."

"No problem," Clarissa said, picking up her drumstick.

They ate in silence a moment then Abby said, "I'll drive to Penticton or Vancouver or wherever Jade is going and I'll tell him how I feel."

"How about you call him first?" Clarissa said.

Abby nodded, her mouth full of chicken, and her heart full of hope.

CHAPTER TWENTY-EIGHT

ABBY CLEARED HER THROAT and waited for the answering service to beep so she could leave a message. She'd hoped to talk to Jade in person but this would have to do since he hadn't picked up.

The sun shone bright as she walked around the park, looking for some shade. She didn't want to go back home, in case her mother was there.

There was silence on the line.

"Oh, hi," Abby said. "This is Abby. I was thinking... Um, I know you think that my life is here, marrying Ben and being near my parents, and that living here is what's best for me, but I don't think it is. I want to be with you." Abby paused. "I know you'll want to spend most of your time with your mom if she's sick and I totally understand. I'd still like to go to Penticton for the rest of the summer, just for a vacation. If that's where you'll be then maybe we can hang out when you get a chance." Abby sighed. Was she being too pushy?

An annoying beeping sound from an incoming call was making it hard to concentrate. "I know there's no immediate future for us," Abby continued, "and that's fine, I just want to spend more time with you."

The beeping continued on, interrupting her thoughts. She looked at her phone screen. Jade's name was on the call display. She quickly answered the call.

"Hello?"

"Abby? Were you calling me just now?" At the sound of his voice Abby almost dropped her phone. How could she miss him this much when it hadn't even been a full day?

"I was just leaving you a message," she said.

"Do you forgive me?" Jade sounded worried.

"Forgive you? For what?"

"For leaving you behind. For acting like my dad and pretending I know anything about what the right thing is to do. I just wanted to protect you from everything going on in my life right now. I don't want you to ever be sad."

"I won't be sad."

He was worried about *her* being sad?

"If your mom is sick," Abby said, "she needs you right now. I understand why you changed your mind about inviting me to go with you." She shut her eyes tight, waiting for his response. There was no answer on the other line.

"Jade?"

"My mom just wants me to have fun and not worry. That's why we're on this vacation and I'm with the youth group. It's not because of her that I told you not to come. I just don't want to drag you into my problems. I don't want to be selfish and bring you with me just because I love… hanging out with you."

"Then let *me* be selfish and follow you."

There was another pause before Jade responded.

"What about Ben?"

"The engagement's over. I called him first before calling you. I never loved Ben."

"But does he love you?"

"No. I really don't think he does."

There was another pause and Abby got the feeling Jade wanted to say something more but was having a hard time saying it. "Is there something else?" she asked. "Something that you are worried about?"

There was another long pause before Jade replied. "It's hard to talk about," his voice sounded strained. "I don't want to be the guy that everyone feels sorry for, especially not with you. And if you knew everything that's going on, then you'd just feel bad... and feel sorry for me."

"Then don't tell me and I won't feel sorry for you."

"But... I should."

"What would make you happiest?" Abby stopped pacing around the large tree at the park. "If you want to talk about it, I'll listen. I'm not going to run away because things aren't perfect and happy in your life. But if you don't want to talk about it, then don't. I still want to be here for you."

"What would make me happiest is to pretend everything is fine and to be with you as long as I can before..." Jade stopped.

"Then that's what we'll do," Abby said. Deep inside, she knew it wouldn't be that simple.

"You have no idea how much I wish you were here right now."

Abby smiled. "I'll see how fast I can get there."

CHAPTER TWENTY-NINE

"**T**HANK YOU SO MUCH, CLARISSA," Abby said, hugging her best friend. She'd driven over four hours to bring Abby to the campground in Creston, where Jade had stopped for the night. He'd gotten halfway to Penticton when he saw Abby's call coming in and stopped at the nearest place, which was Creston, to call her back.

"I owe you big time," Abby said to Clarissa, letting go of her.

"You don't owe me. I did it for *looove*." Clarissa made a kissy face and Abby laughed. She got her backpack and sleeping bag from the back seat of the car.

"How are you feeling?" Clarissa asked.

"Nervous. Wide awake. A little nauseous."

"I think it's so romantic that you're following your heart."

"You always follow your heart, too," Abby said, closing the car door.

"No, that's not exactly what I follow," Clarissa said out the car window.

Abby rolled her eyes. "Wish me luck."

"Good luck," Clarissa leaned through the open window. "Are you sure you wouldn't rather stay in a hotel room with me tonight and meet up with Jade in the morning?"

Abby hesitated. "No, I can camp." She smiled, but inside her tummy fluttered. Could she camp? She had never camped before.

"Okay then, have fun!" Clarissa waved goodbye then drove away, honking the horn as the car tires kicked up a cloud of dust down the drive.

Abby watched the car disappear around the corner. Could she really do this? Could she really just be carefree and do a road trip with Jade? They'd sleep in the same tent, have breakfast, lunch and supper together. Well, at least until they reached Penticton.

Then what? She'd have to find some kind of temporary job for a few weeks if she wanted to stay there for the rest of the summer.

Abby shook her head. She wouldn't get ahead of herself. She'd take it one day at a time. And she wasn't going to use her parents' credit card or they'd know where she was. She didn't want her mom to know where she was. Not yet. She shouldn't have to report her whereabouts to her mother, like she was a child.

Turning away from the street to the campground office, Abby headed down the gravel road that led to the campsites. The tiny rocks crunched beneath her shoes as she walked. Nestled in the trees at the center of the campground, past the R.V. area, were all the tenting sites.

There was more lighting near the center, which made Abby feel better. It was already dark and the trees towered over her, making her feel small and vulnerable.

The washroom building was built like a cabin with wooden steps leading up to the entrances on either side. Flower baskets hung from the roof's edge and a flower bed of colourful carnations ran along the front of the building. It was all very quaint and welcoming.

Abby passed by a small stage with a rounded half-dome roof that was decorated with tiny lights and Patio lanterns. In front of the stage was an open area with a volley ball net and a small wooden playground for kids. Two little girls chased each other around the swings and a group of older kids zoomed by on their bicycles, kicking up dust as they went.

Abby walked slowly past each site, looking for Jade's car. She was getting more and more excited to see him but the nervous feeling in her stomach slowed her down. What would she say when she saw him?

Then she saw Jade's small blue car, hidden on the other side of the washroom building, with one lonely tent beside it. A power cord ran out from the tent to an outlet built into a short wooden post. From inside the tent a blue light shone.

Setting her backpack and sleeping bag down, Abby approached the tent. "Jade?"

Jade took her by surprise, pulling her onto the sleeping bag inside. Abby squealed. A foam mattress cushioned her fall as she landed onto her back.

"You actually came!" Jade said. Before she could answer him he kissed her, his hands around her waist. With a small grunt Abby rolled on top of him and kissed him back. She'd been waiting for this all day.

Jade chuckled, moving her hair out of her face and tucking it behind her ears. He kissed her again, more slowly this time, his hand trailing down her back and over her bottom. Even through her jean shorts she could feel his light touches.

She sighed and their tongues touched, making her ache for more. She wasn't sure for what exactly, just *more*. She pushed up against Jade and kissed him harder.

"Abby, wait," he said between kisses. "Slow down." He smoothed back her hair from her face again. It kept falling down. Something hard in Jade's pocket, like a flashlight, was rubbing uncomfortably against Abby's leg and now that they'd stopped for a moment she was getting annoyed with it and wanted to move it.

"Ouch," she said, reaching down to grab the object. "What is this?"

Jade inhaled a quick sharp breath when she closed her hand around it. He gently moved her hand aside and sat up, his eyes shining in the light of his laptop screen. Abby got up too, suddenly realizing where her hand had been.

"Oh," her cheeks grew hot. "Sorry." She wanted to crawl under the blankets and hide, and never come out again.

"I just…" Jade cleared his throat. "I've never had sex before." He lifted her chin so she would look at him. "But it's kind of obvious you haven't either."

He gave her a kiss on the cheek then climbed out of the tent. "I'll be right back," he said, looking back through the tent entrance. "I just need to splash some cold water on my face or something."

Abby nodded, her cheeks growing even hotter. When Jade was gone she lay down onto his sleeping bag. This was going to be a long night.

CHAPTER THIRTY

ABBY LAY HER HEAD DOWN onto Jade's pillow and pulled her knees up, hugging them to her chest. The more she kissed him, the more she wanted *more*. Would it ever be enough? Her body was practically vibrating with desire. But 'more' wasn't an option.

Nothing had ever, or would ever fit inside of her. It was her embarrassing secret she'd been hiding all of her life, not wanting anyone to know she was defective. She'd never had a reason to tell anyone or deal with it before. But now...

Abby sat up, a sudden thought hitting her. Did Jade think they would have sex? It was the natural progresssion of things, right? So maybe he thought her deciding to come with him meant they'd have sex at some point, especially since she was older. Was she misleading him?

She climbed out of the tent just as Jade was returning into it.

"Whoa," he said as she bumped into him. He held out a hand to steady her. "Everything okay?"

"I can't have sex with you!" she blurted out.

A curly-haired woman with glasses looked over at them then walked faster, hurrying into the washroom building.

"I mean," Abby said more quietly. "Not that I can't have sex with *you* specifically."

Jade held his hands up in surrender. "Okay, no worries." He smiled and Abby relaxed a little. "No sex. Understood, I promise."

"It's not you." A lump formed in Abby's throat. If there was ever anyone she'd want to get that close to it would be Jade. Now he probably thought she didn't desire him. But she did, so much, and if she wasn't abnormal the way she was then she'd let things progress between them.

"Really, it's not you," she said, avoiding looking at him. "I just can't have sex, with anyone. I thought you should know that."

There it was, the same thing she'd told Ben. His rejection hit her now full force, a week delayed. She winced, waiting for a similar rejection from Jade this time.

"Why are you so worried about it?" Jade said. "It's fine." He pulled her into a gentle hug. "I hope I didn't make you feel pressured."

"No, you didn't." Abby sank into his embrace. Then the tears flowed. She couldn't help it. With all the driving that day and tension at home between her and her mother and then the sexual frustration of just moments ago, she couldn't hold back the tears any longer. Why couldn't she be normal like everyone else and just have sex? It was the most natural and easy thing to do. Girls didn't even have to *do* anything during the process, just lie there and be available.

"I'm sorry," Jade said, running his hand over her hair. Abby wanted to tell him it wasn't his fault, but she was too choked up to talk. "Are you worried that's why

I changed my mind about you coming along with me?" Jade asked. "Because I was hoping we'd have sex?"

Abby nodded.

"Well, that's not why. That's kind of the furthest thing from my mind right now." Jade rubbed her back gently. "Well, not when we were in the tent, but I mean lately." He stopped, his heart beating fast beneath Abby's cheek. "I couldn't stop thinking about you the whole drive and then when you called I was so happy. I really need…" Abby waited for him to continue. Was he choked up with emotion too?

"I just really need you right now," he finally said. Abby hugged him tighter.

Despite the late hour the campground was alive with people moving about and gathering around the small camp fires that were at each site. In the near distance the forest trees stood like a wall of darkness. Yet in Jade's arms, Abby felt safe. There was nowhere else in the world she would rather be.

"Just a second, I'll be right back." She wiped her tears away and ran to her backpack to get her earbuds from one of the front pockets.

"Here." She handed one to Jade and plugged the earphones into her cell phone, selecting a romantic song. She took the other earbud for herself.

"Thanks," Jade smiled. "Good song."

"I never went to the high school dances," Abby said, turning up the volume. "But this place is so romantic, with the patio lanterns, I was just thinking—"

"Abby," Jade put a finger on her lips to stop her from talking, "will you dance with me?"

Abby nodded and he set his hands on her hips.

They danced beneath the little lights, their bodies moving together in a slow rhythm. Jade's hands slid beneath Abby's shirt, cool against her lower back.

They danced as the kids around them rode their bikes and people walked to and from the washrooms.

They danced until the movement around them became less and less and the temperature dropped.

"Let's go lie down," Jade whispered when Abby shivered in his arms. His breath was close to her ear and it sent a wave of heat down her side. She tensed at the thought of sleeping with Jade. But they'd already fallen asleep together on the couch the other day, so why did this seem different? She pulled away from him, a cold draft coming between them.

"I'm too tired to change into pajamas," she said, putting her phone and earbuds into her pocket. It wasn't a lie, she was exhausted, but it was more of an excuse not to get too undressed, not yet.

"Me too," Jade said, although he didn't look tired.

Cuddled together in the tent a few minutes later, Abby fell asleep in Jade's arms, listening to the sound of the traffic on the highway somewhere beyond the campground trees.

CHAPTER THIRTY-ONE

I T WAS IMPOSSIBLE TO SLEEP IN, with all the birds chattering and campers moving about outside. The tent walls were no barrier to the sounds of these early risers. The air smelled fresh in the early morning, mixed with the enticing aroma of bacon and campfire smoke. Abby's stomach growled.

She lay awake on her back, beside Jade, who was still asleep. She glanced over at him. What would it feel like to wake up the morning after you lost your virginity to the person you loved? It must be a pretty good feeling, like you could do anything now. No longer just a bystander of the happy, sexually active couples all around you.

Abby breathed in slowly. She'd already come a long way, letting down the walls she'd built up all her life to keep men out. Eventually guys always wanted to have sex and she'd get hurt in the end, when they would leave.

But it was different with Jade. In the beginning there was no pressure, no expectations. Maybe that's why she'd let down her guard. And now she wanted more.

Did this mean she might finally be ready to deal with her 'problem'? The truth was she could have made more of an effort to find a solution in the past, she just never had any real motivation to, not until now.

"Good morning," Jade said, bringing her out of her thoughts. His voice was hoarse with sleep. Abby turned onto her side to face him.

"Good morning," she smiled.

He reached over and put his hand on hers. "Did you sleep okay?"

"Yes. I was just up early."

Jade took out his cell phone. "It's still early."

"Do you think you would feel different, after having sex?" Abby asked.

"Different?" Jade turned onto his side and looked at her. "Like physically or emotionally?"

"Both."

"For a guy... I'd think maybe they'd feel different emotionally, like proud of themselves or something."

Abby huffed. "Like they scored?"

Jade shrugged. "I guess. If it was a conquest. But I don't think it's that way for every guy. It would feel special if the girl was important to him." Jade turned onto his back again, looking up at the tent ceiling. Abby moved in close and cuddled up. He played with her hair and was quiet.

"Sorry. That's kind of a dumb question to ask."

"No, it's not," he smoothed her hair back. "I'd be really happy, knowing that I found someone I loved enough to want to try that with."

Abby rested her hand on Jade's chest, playing with his t-shirt. "You mentioned your parents being religious. Are you?"

He didn't answer.

"I was just curious."

"When I was eight," Jade began, "my best friend was having a Star Wars party for his birthday and we were both really excited..." he inhaled slowly, his chest rising beneath Abby's hand. "What he wanted more than anything was this cool lightsaber that came out from the base at the push of a button, glowed and made sound effects. But it was really expensive.

"My parents never had a lot of extra money but I convinced them to get it for Scott. When I saw it in the box I wanted one so bad, but I also wanted Scott to have it. I could hardly wait to see him open his present."

Jade stopped talking and Abby wondered if that was the end of his story. But she waited.

"Then," Jade continued, "I got really sick and there was no way I was going to get better in time to go to Scott's birthday party. I remember being mad at my parents, mad at God, and then finally realizing I had no real control over anything in my life.

"To make a long story short, I prayed every night that I wouldn't miss the party, even though the doctor said there was no way I'd be out of the hospital that fast. But I got better, faster than I should have, and I got to go to the party.

"I ended up getting a lightsaber too, which was something I didn't think was important enough to even mention in prayer, but I did anyway, and Scottie got two of the same lightsabers for his birthday. He gave me one so we could play together. We played with them every day after school.

"But now, there are things I've prayed for, things way more important than a lightsaber, that I haven't gotten and I don't understand..."

Jade stopped a moment, squeezing Abby's shoulders with the arm he held her with.

"So, to answer your question is no, I don't think I'm all that religious anymore. I can't remember the last time I prayed."

Abby thought about this. She couldn't really relate but she could understand his need to believe in something. "I had an imaginary friend when I was eight," she said. "My mom didn't like it at all."

She smiled against Jade's chest, remembering how annoyed her mother would get whenever Abby talked to her imaginary friend. "It was fun but I think believing in God would be more special, because it's like someone is actually listening. But my parents were never religious, so I guess I never was either."

"I don't think I was religious because my dad was a pastor. I didn't even like his sermons." Jade kissed her forehead. "You're right, there's something magical about believing when you're a kid."

"I would have liked it. But I guess it's too late for me to believe in all that now."

"That's not true..." Jade put his free hand over his eyes. "Never mind. Sorry." He sat up. "Let's not talk about this anymore." He had tears in his eyes that he was trying to hide.

Abby's heart squeezed in her chest. She made a mental note never to ask him about religion again. It was obviously a painful topic. He lay back down with a sigh.

"Tell me about your problems," he said.

"My problems?"

"Yes." He got up on one elbow and looked down at her. "You said you can't have sex with anyone, *ever*. Do you have plans to join a convent or some-thing?"

"No." Abby hugged her arms around herself, curling her legs up to her chest. "It's just that some-thing's wrong... with me." Suddenly it was like she lost all control over the words that poured out of her mouth.

"I'm useless," she said, wrapping her arms around her face. "I can't even do something as simple and natural and basic to all humanity as have sex." She turned away from Jade, clenching her fists tight and forcing herself not to cry. She had never disliked herself more than she did at that moment.

"What do you mean?" Jade put a hand on her shoulder and she pulled away.

"It's just so stupid, I can't..." Abby shook her head and swallowed hard. "I can't..." She took a moment to breathe. She'd started the sentence so she would finish it. "I can't get anything inside there. I honestly don't even know how I get my period." She shoved her face into her pillow. "Never mind, I'm just abnormal, okay?"

Jade didn't reply and she was too embarrassed to face him. A moment later she heard him typing away on his laptop. She looked up to see what he was doing. He was searching online.

"What are you searching for?" she asked, wiping her tears away.

"I doubt you're the only one in the world with this problem." He faced the screen away from her curious gaze. "Not sure what I'll find, so..."

"My dad always says to look for a government website when you need answers, it will have logical information and stats."

Jade burst out laughing, surprising Abby. Then she laughed too.

"I think I found a good site." Jade wiped his tears of laughter away. "But it's not government of Canada issued. Is that okay?"

Abby stuck her tongue out at him.

"Testimonials, here we go." He looked back at the screen. "Kathy says, I feel like a failure. Why can't I have sex? The worst part is how it has affected my relationship with my boyfriend. I have never been able to let him inside me..."

"Let me see." Abby moved in closer to look at the screen. "Joanne says," she read, "we were both virgins and waited until marriage to have sex. But on our honeymoon we were surprised to find that we couldn't consummate. I had always suspected that my vagina was too small, because I could never insert a tampon no matter how hard I tried. My doctor told me that I just needed to try harder. We have tried countless times yet any attempt to push the..." Abby skipped that part. "Nothing that I have read about sex says anything about this." She stopped reading.

Jade looked at her. "Does any of this sound like you?"

"I guess."

He scrolled down the page. "I'm just browsing through this page about Vaginismus. Have you heard of that?"

Abby shook her head.

"It says, Vaginismus is an involuntary contraction of the muscles surrounding the entrance to the vagina, making penetration impossible or painful." Jade glanced over at her for a second then continued reading. "Here are some questions. Have you ever been sexually abused?"

"No."

"Are you afraid of pregnancy?"

"Very much so."

"Do you have high anxiety?"

"Sort of. It used to be much worse."

"Violence in the home?"

"Not physical."

"Inadequate sex education?"

"Probably."

"Overly strict or unbalanced religious teaching?"

"No. But my mom is strict."

"Fear of pain?"

"Yes."

"Well, they've got a book called '10 steps to completely overcoming Vaginismus'. Or you can get the self-help package. It says it has a ninety percent success rate."

"What's in the package?"

"It costs one hundred dollars for the books and products."

"One hundred dollars?" Abby frowned. She wouldn't be able to afford the program, but her insides fluttered at the thought of there being an actual solution to her problem. Would it really work? Was her situation as simple as muscle spasms and illogical fears?

"I have a PayPal account," Jade said, clicking around. "I sold a bunch of my stuff and there's money in there now." He clicked on the checkout button. "Just gotta find the mailing address to the campground in Penticton."

"Wait." If he bought the package then…

"Done!" Jade sat up. "Express shipping to the Skaha Campground." He gave Abby a kiss on the lips. "I'm going to have a quick shower and then we'll go eat. I'm starving." He left before Abby could gather her thoughts enough to form a reply.

CHAPTER THIRTY-TWO

THE DOOR TO THE GIRLS' WASHROOM was propped open with a garbage can when Abby went in. Someone was taking a shower in one of the stalls, fogging up all the bathroom mirrors.

While waiting for Jade to shower, she'd decided to take one herself. This would be her first time showering at a campground washroom. It seemed so open and public, even with the doors on the stalls.

She went in, clutching her change of clothes and bathroom stuff. The floor had a wooden grate covering the cement below.

She removed her shoes and stepped onto the wooden floor, then closed the small latch on the door and began to undress.

A cool draft blew over her bare skin, making Abby feel exposed, like she was changing outdoors. It was kind of exciting and stimulating too. She stepped under the shower head and pulled the curtain closed. She could take her time and not have to worry about using all the hot water, like she did at her apartment.

Standing back, she turned the taps and set the temperature. The hot water pinched her skin and cascaded over her long hair then down her body, tickling her bare bottom. She let her hands follow the path of the water, trailing over her breasts, noticing how they felt to touch, how they would feel to Jade if he were to touch them. She let out a small gasp, then quickly took her hands away.

There was no point in wasting time in the shower. Jade was probably waiting for her now. She washed her hair and body then rinsed off. When she stepped out of the shower, a cold draft greeted her.

Shivering, she stepped back in. Why was she in a hurry anyway? Was it her parents that had made her so reserved about her body? They'd never said anything bad about sex, or had they? Her mother's disapproving looks came to mind. She remembered a couple times when her questions were met with displeased glances and frustrated sighs, like the topic was inappropriate.

Then she'd met Clarissa, who was so free and uninhibited, nothing at all like Abby. Would she always be like this? Would she ever change?

Abby decided to stay under the hot water for a bit longer and fill the washroom building with more steam. Why not?

She turned up the heat even more, tilting her head back and soaping herself again with lots of shower gel to make bubbles. The hot water felt so good. She squeezed her Loofah over her chest and let the foam trail down her body, making her slippery all over. Then she ran her hands over her breasts and tummy.

She imagined Jade's hands gliding all over her and her thoughts jumped back to the previous night in the tent when she'd accidentally touched him. It was embarrassing, but not as scary as it would have been with anyone else. She was curious about his body, too, but only his and no one else's. He put her at ease and she trusted him.

Abby slid her hand down past her bellybutton and below. If she could just relax a bit, maybe the muscles would open up and...

She slid her fingers farther down.

CHAPTER THIRTY-THREE

"**A**RE YOU OKAY?" Jade asked, fidgeting with the small wine menu on the table.

He sat across from Abby in a booth at a downtown diner. The ceiling and walls of the restaurant were made of wood, giving the place a cozy cabin feel to it.

A large moose head hung above the bar and heavy blinds on the windows kept the bright sun out. The only other customers were two older gentlemen sitting at the bar, both eating in silence.

"Abby?" Jade reached over and placed his hand on hers. "Will you tell me what's wrong?"

"I'm fine," Abby replied, setting her lips in a tight line. She'd been silent the entire time they'd packed up the tent at the campground and then while driving through town in search of a place to eat.

Jade hadn't asked any questions, but now he looked concerned. Maybe he thought it was something he'd done to upset her. But she wasn't mad at him. She was mad at herself.

"What'll you be having?" A middle aged waitress with a smoker's voice said loudly, startling them both.

"Can we look at a menu?" Jade asked.

"Oh, sure." She grabbed two menus from the bar and returned. "Folks usually just order the eggs, hash browns and bacon."

"Then that's what I'll have." Jade smiled at her and she seemed to brighten up.

"Sure thing." She pulled out her notepad. "And for the young lady?"

"An eggs Benedict?" Abby said, not sure why it had come out as a question.

"I'll see what I can do." The waitress winked at them and left.

Jade looked back to Abby again, his smile fading. "Are you upset that I ordered that self-help package for you?"

"No." Abby shook her head. "It's really sweet that you are trying to help me, but it's useless."

She slumped down in the cushioned seat, letting go of Jade's hand. "I hate my body."

"Don't say that." He leaned forward onto the table, speaking softly. "Remember those testimonials? They all got through it, right?"

"Ninety percent of them, not all."

"But that's a really good success rate."

"What if I end up one of the ten percent who doesn't succeed?"

"You won't," Jade said. Abby wished she could be as confident as he was, but knowing her luck, she'd be one of the unsuccessful ten percent. It wasn't just her muscles that were the problem, she also had her anxiety issue that she'd be working around all of her life. That had to be part of the problem too.

"I tried." Abby looked down at the table. "Today, in the shower..." She stopped, too embarrassed to continue.

Jade seemed to think about this for a moment. "It's an involuntary reaction right?" he said. "Like your eye automatically closing when something gets close to it. It's not something that is wrong with you." When Abby didn't reply Jade continued. "You can't just shove a finger into your eye. It will close tighter."

"You two talking about contact lenses?" The waitress said, returning with two coffees they hadn't ordered. She set them down onto the table. "I know when I first got contact lenses I could barely put them in. My eyes kept watering. You just have to keep practicing."

Abby nodded silently, holding back a smile.

"It's not easy," the waitress continued. "You just gotta keep trying until you get used to it. It's just a natural reflex, so you have to teach yourself to keep that eye open."

She opened one eye wide as though to demonstrate. "Imagine how many things would get into your eye if you had no reflexes to block them out, bugs, sand, water…"

Jade grimaced and Abby giggled.

The waitress lifted an eyebrow at them. "You two all right?"

Abby and Jade both nodded and the waitress left. When she was out of earshot they burst out laughing.

After breakfast they were back in the car, driving towards the mountains. Jade turned on the music and Abby settled back into her seat. It felt good to be on the way to Penticton again. They'd be there before suppertime if they didn't stop along the way. She could hardly wait to get back to the sun, the beach and the festive atmosphere.

But how would she pay for this vacation? Her smile dwindled as she looked out the car window. Maybe she could get a job at one of the vendor booths at the beach for a couple hours a day.

She glanced at Jade. He seemed deep in thought too as he drove. The road turned left, then right, winding through the mountains. A wall of rock ran along one side and on the other was a steep cliff drop.

A fog had settled onto the mountain and Abby was glad she couldn't see how high up they were. She opened her window and a rush of fresh mountain air wafted in. Here, it was easy to believe in a higher power that created it all.

Abby rested her head back against the seat. Maybe if she prayed for a job in Penticton she'd find one. Her mind wandered as she thought of what she could do for temporary work and soon she dozed off to the sounds of the radio.

Abby dreamed that she accidentally stepped on Bailey's tail and the little dog yelped. She woke to the sound, only it wasn't Bailey but the car tires screeching as Jade slammed on the breaks.

A group of mountain goats stood frozen at the center of the road, eyes wide and staring back at them. Abby's seatbelt dug into her chest, holding her back as the car swerved and spun out of control. It went up onto two wheels for a terrifying moment.

Abby thrust her hands out in front of her onto the dash, fighting against the forward momentum that strained her neck.

The smell of burning rubber filled the car. A blur of goats and the grey rock face of the mountain side passed in front of the windshield. Then came the jolt of the hood smashing into rock and a sickening metal crunch sound.

Then silence.

It all happened so fast. A ringing in Abby's ears filled the silence. The crushed hood in front of the shattered windshield hissed and steamed.

"Jade?" Abby said. Her voice sounded distant and her throat felt like she'd swallowed sand. She tried to turn her head to look at Jade, but her neck cramped up, so she stopped. *Oh God,* she gripped the dashboard, breathing hard. *Take me, not Jade.*

There was a groan from the driver's seat. "I'm okay," Jade grunted. He was moving now and Abby relaxed.

"I think I blacked out for a second," Jade continued. "Are you okay?"

Abby was in too much of a shock to respond. They could have died, just like that.

Jade took her hand in his. "Are you hurt?"

Tears streaked down her cheeks. "We're still alive."

"Yeah," Jade said softly. "I guess we are."

CHAPTER THIRTY-FOUR

"**I** JUST REALIZED THAT CRASHING my car was on my bucket list," Jade said as he struggled with the hotel room key. It was the middle of the night and they were standing in front of the door to a dingy motel room. "Not that I did it on purpose." He turned to Abby. "I would never put you into any danger, I'd rather die first."

"Don't say that," Abby said, yawning. This was the day that just wouldn't end. They'd spent hours waiting for a tow truck and more hours at a clinic being checked over. Other than bruises beneath one breast at her ribs because of the seatbelt, Abby was fine.

Jade had mild whiplash but otherwise was okay too. He'd refused to call his parents. He didn't want to worry them and the car was his anyway. Abby didn't call her parents either.

They hitchhiked instead and a trucker picked them up. He offered to drive them all night but Jade insisted they stop at the nearest hotel. He wasn't feeling well. The trucker dropped them off at a dingy motel in the middle of nowhere on the lonely highway.

Abby was too tired to complain about the place, or even to be scared to stay at such a small motel hidden in the shadows of a massive forest. She just wanted to sleep.

Crickets chirped loudly as she waited for Jade to open the door. They were louder than any she'd ever heard before. Where they bigger out here in the forest?

"Everything okay?" Abby asked, moving in closer to Jade.

"I didn't know there were any hotels left that still used real keys instead of swipe cards," Jade said.

"Motel," Abby corrected. "Are you still feeling sick?"

"I'm fine, just need to take some medicine." He finally got the door open and stepped aside for Abby to enter. She headed straight for the bed and collapsed onto it. A cloud of dust rose from the comforter.

Abby sneezed. "This is the most run down motel I've ever seen, in real life or in the movies."

Jade laughed and set his suitcase down beside her backpack. Then he locked the deadbolt on the door.

"Welcome to our honeymoon suite!" He flipped on the light switch.

Abby groaned, covering her eyes with her arm to block out the yellowish light. "I feel like I got run over by a truck. Twice. I'm so tired I think I'm going to stop breathing soon."

"Wow, I really hope you don't." Jade rummaged through his luggage and Abby heard the sound of a pill bottle.

"Headache?" she asked.

"Something like that."

Abby uncovered her eyes and looked over at him. He had a medicine container in his hand that had a label printed on the orange bottle. He went into the washroom before Abby could ask if it was a prescription. Was he sick? Abby's stomach tightened. Would it be rude to ask?

She heard the sound of water running in the washroom. Maybe it was for headaches. If so, she'd probably need one soon. She closed her eyes.

"You look tense," Jade said when he returned. He climbed onto the bed beside her. "I have a degree in massage therapy."

"You do?" Abby perked up, raising her head off the bed to look at Jade.

"No. But can I give you a massage anyway?" He sat on the side of the bed. The cheap mattress tilted so that Abby rolled towards him. He caught her before she fell onto the floor.

"I think this bed is trying to tell us something," he said, helping Abby sit up.

"That we should get into our pajamas and go to sleep before I die of tiredness?" she asked.

"Yes," Jade kissed her. It was becoming something of a habit now—him stealing kisses every chance he got. "Are you sure you're tired? Because you don't look tired."

"Oh really?" Abby said against Jade's lips. "How do I look?"

"Delicious."

Abby laughed. "No one's ever called me delicious before."

Jade kissed her again and Abby pulled back. "Let me get into my pajamas," she said. "Then I wouldn't mind kissing some more."

"Okay." He helped her off the bed. "But if you're not back soon I might just fall asleep."

Abby rolled her eyes and headed into the washroom. It was quite small and the walls were painted in brown and yellow, which matched the stains in the bathtub. Good thing she'd showered at the campground that morning. Hopefully the bed sheets were well bleached.

Undressing to her bra and underwear, she realized that her backpack with her pajamas was still in the other room. The thought of putting her jeans back on was too exhausting. Jade had already seen her in a bikini before anyway.

Opening the door slowly, Abby peeked out. Jade was lying on the bed with his laptop open. He didn't look up when she walked out into the room.

She stood there a moment, observing him. He had a thin black t-shirt on that hugged his lean body. His dark hair hung into his blue eyes and the light from the computer screen accented his strong jaw. His long legs stretched out behind him on the small bed, over the side, and the muscles in his arms twitched as he typed. He shifted, pulling the laptop closer to himself.

Abby got her backpack quickly but Jade glanced up before she could retreat back to the bathroom. He looked pleasantly surprised to see her undressed. His eyes traveled down the length of her body. She forced herself to stay where she was despite the urge to go run and hide. This wasn't any different than wearing a bikini at the beach. But then why did it feel so different?

Jade jumped up from the bed and walked over to her. His physical reaction was becoming quickly noticeable. Abby's cheeks flushed and she looked away. It seemed inappropriate to stare.

Jade touched her arm. "Do you need help getting into your pajamas?" he asked, his voice husky.

Abby couldn't decide. She could let him undress her and finally give in, finally let go. A part of her wanted to, desperately.

Jade's hand trailed down her arm then back up again. "You're shaking."

"Just chilly," Abby said, even though that wasn't the reason at all.

"I've never seen a girl in her bra before. In real life that is," Jade said softly, looking down at her breasts.

"Well, I've never stood in front of a guy in my bra before," Abby said. She swallowed hard, refusing to feel insecure about her body. Her heart beating fast, she reached behind her and undid the clasp of her bra. A small grin worked its way onto Jade's lips. He studied her eyes as though searching for an answer to an unspoken question.

Abby let go of the clasp.

CHAPTER THIRTY-FIVE

THUNDER RUMBLED IN THE DISTANCE as Abby stood there, waiting for Jade to do something. Anything. The moment stretched on as he seemed to consider what to do next. Abby gave him a smile and that seemed to help him decide.

He reached up and slipped one bra strap off her shoulder, then the other and removed her bra. Her breath caught as her nipples hardened in cool air.

Jade looked down, his gaze caressing her.

Abby waited a second for him to look then reached around his neck and kissed him, pushing her chest against his warm t-shirt. He kissed her back, then stepped away only long enough to pull his t-shirt over his head and bring her close again.

She relaxed at the sensation of his warm skin against hers. He picked her up and lay her onto the bed. The cold comforter scratched at her back but she didn't care. Jade climbed on top of her and she arched upward, impatient for him to lower himself onto her.

He kissed her heatedly, running his hand along the side of her breast and down her body. Then he abandoned her lips and kissed her neck. Abby tilted her head to the side.

Jade's hands trembled as they roamed over her breasts and down to her tummy, then back to her breasts again.

Taking his hand, Abby placed his palm over her nipple. He sighed against her lips and grasped her breast, squeezing it lightly. His tongue traced her top lip as he ran his thumb over her nipple in a circular motion, making her imagine his tongue there. The throbbing between her legs was unbearable.

"Jade," she whimpered, aching for him. But she wasn't ready to have sex, not after the failed attempt at getting her finger in during her shower that morning.

"Abby don't whimper like that," Jade whispered against her lips. "I can't keep... holding back." He rolled off of her and lay on his back, catching his breath. His jeans looked uncomfortably tight. Abby reached over and undid the top button.

"Thank you." He sighed in relief, running a hand through his hair. She could now see his boxers.

Reaching over, she clasped her hand around the fabric, curious if the width was as thick as she remember-ed from the day before, when she'd accidentally grabbed him in the tent.

It was.

How would something this thick fit inside of her? Jade moaned at her touch and closed his eyes. At least he didn't mind her exploration. She couldn't believe how hard it was. She squeezed and Jade sucked in a short breath.

"Sorry, does that hurt?" she asked.

"No," he said quickly, shaking his head.

Abby released her grip and his muscles contracted, moving in a way that surprised her, like this part of his body had a life of its own. She tried squeezing it again and the same thing happened. She was about to do it again when Jade grabbed her wrist to stop her. In one swift movement he was on top of her, his breath ragged and fingers warm and clammy as he touched her face, then her hair, kissing her urgently.

"Abby I'm going to..." he kept smoothing her hair back, the strands getting caught in his fingers. He curled them into a fist, pulling her head back. He was hard against her abdomen so she shifted to the side, offering her hip bone instead. He thrust forward and a warmth spread over her hip. She wrapped her legs around him, wanting to reach a climax too. But Jade untangled from her and rolled away.

"I'm sorry," he said, seeming embarrassed. He got up quickly and headed into the bathroom. "I'm just going to get cleaned up."

Abby lay on the bed, naked except for her panties, and trembling with desire. She rolled onto her belly, the cool of the blanket beneath her breasts arousing her to her last point of resolve. She couldn't wait any longer. Grabbing a pillow from underneath the blanket she wrapped her legs around it and squeezed.

She held back a cry of pleasure as the muscles inside of her contracted and spasmed in a very satisfying way. Then she sighed, going limp and releasing the pillow.

"Abby!" Jade said from behind her. She looked up at him. "Next time let me help you with that," he said, pulling her into sitting position. "Put this on before you catch a cold." He held out her pajamas and she wondered how long he'd been out of the washroom while she was squeezing that pillow.

"It's not that cold in here," she said. "I kind of like the feeling of being topless."

"Then put it on before I jump on you again," Jade said, holding the shirt up for her to put on.

"What do you mean, next time to let you help me? With what?" Abby put her arms through the arm holes of the fleece top and Jade pulled it closed at the front.

"With an orgasm." He kissed her on the lips then began to button up her shirt. The soft fabric made her feel safe and warm. And so did Jade's careful movements. *He* made her feel safe, like she could do anything when she was with him.

243

"I've never had anyone help me with that before," she said, letting him button up the fleece top, even though she could have done it herself.

"Neither have I," Jade said. Their eyes met and he gave her a lopsided grin. He picked up the pajama bottoms and she put her feet into them. "Other than now of course," he said, helping her pull the bottoms up.

"I didn't exactly help you."

"You've been teasing me for days." There was a glint in his eyes.

"I have?"

"Not on purpose. But I've been wanting to be close to you since the moment I met you." He pulled her onto the bed with him and they snuggled close together.

"I feel better," Abby sighed. "I think I really needed that."

"Which part?"

"The pillow part."

"Oh." Jade sounded disappointed.

"I mean the part where you were touching me all over," Abby said, looking up at him. She couldn't help but smile. He was just too adorable.

"How can you orgasm without anything inside of you?" he asked.

"I don't know. It's easy." Abby's cheeks flushed at her quick reply. It was something about herself she hadn't even told Clarissa. Maybe because she knew Clarissa had a hard time with having orgasms, despite her sexually active lifestyle.

"I'm sorry if I disrespected you," Jade said, a serious expression on his face.

"You didn't disrespect me," she reassured him. "I'm the one who walked out of the washroom in my bra and panties, remember?"

"I'm not... like that, you know, with girls. I just kind of lost my," he shook his head. "I don't know, sorry."

Abby wrapped her arms around him. "I know you're not like that." She buried her head into his shoulder, wishing he didn't feel guilty. She was all too familiar with that feeling, every time her mom disapproved of something she said or did. "I'm not like that, either. Do you want to forget it ever happened?"

"Are you kidding?" Jade rested his hand on her head, smoothing her hair back. "I'd never want to forget that."

"Me neither," Abby whispered, closing her eyes.

"Were you uncomfortable with anything?"

"No, I enjoyed it all. A lot."

Jade's muscles relaxed beneath her touch. It didn't take long for him to fall asleep. The last thing he said was, "one step at a time, Abby. There's no rush. Patience makes the heart grow fonder."

"I thought it was distance that made the heart grow fonder," she'd whispered in return, but he was already asleep.

She stayed awake, replaying the evening over in her mind, not wanting to forget even one small detail.

A new world was opening up before her. A world where going on a honeymoon, making love on Christmas Eve, being a wife, having a family… a world where all of those things were possible.

Her chest filled with emotion and tears came to her eyes. Would having a baby one day be possible for her? The first day of kindergarten, cute Halloween costumes, all the things she'd always thought would never be an option because she was too scared of sharing her body with anyone.

But she wasn't scared around Jade, maybe a little nervous sometimes, but not scared. And she wasn't afraid of his body either, the way she was whenever she saw a photo or diagram of guys' private parts on line. She could never get used to it.

And she wasn't so embarrassed of her body anymore, either. She'd always thought it was working against her. But maybe she just needed to understand it better. The self-help program they ordered online would help with that.

Abby smiled, her thoughts becoming more random as she began to dose off. Being here with Jade felt like a secret place, one that they alone shared. She was almost asleep but then remembered something, her prayer in the car when she thought Jade had been hurt. He was fine and so was she. And she'd never felt more alive than she did when they were touching each other. Would it be wrong to thank God for that, since they weren't married?

Snuggling up close to Jade, Abby closed her eyes, wanting for nothing more than to stay in his arms forever.

CHAPTER THIRTY-SIX

THE AFTERNOON SUN WARMED Abby's face as she walked towards the Skaha Campground. Jade walked beside her carrying two tents, his own and another small one for her, all in one hand. With the other hand he pulled his suitcase behind him. They'd hitch-hiked to Walmart to get a small tent for Abby, before taking a taxi to the campground.

Abby slowed her pace as she walked up the sloped road which led to the office. She wasn't ready yet to give Jade up to his family. But she couldn't be selfish. They needed him more than she did. She glanced over at him as they came to a stop. He hadn't said much in the last hour so she wasn't sure what he was thinking.

"I'll go check in at the office," she said, breaking the silence.

Jade leaned in and kissed her on the lips. "Guess it's time to face the music," he said, handing her the small tent. "I'll text you later and come visit your campsite."

Abby nodded and they parted ways. She headed towards the office and Jade went down the gravel path that lead to the campsites. As she watched him walk away her heart ached. Was it stupid of her to believe they could have a future together? Jade was young and had his whole life ahead of him. She could sense he was unsure about their future too. She only wished she knew exactly why.

With a sigh she climbed up the front steps to the office. The first thing she noticed was the 'help wanted' sign in the window. It seemed a little more than a coincidence. Smiling, she opened the door.

A bell jingled as she stepped into the small office. It was crowded, even with just the few customers that were waiting. Maps covered the walls and local tourist information was scattered everywhere.

"I'll be right with you," the young girl at the front desk said. She smiled at Abby then turned her attention back to the middle aged woman at the front of the line.

"We need a site right away," the woman said. She was wearing a Hawaiian shirt and her hair was as frazzled as she sounded.

"Do you have any sites with hookups left?" A large bald man stepped forward, interrupting them. The woman gave him an angry glare and was about to respond when the front door jingled again and an Italian woman came in.

"There are no toilet paper rolls in any of the stalls and one of the toilets is backed up in the women's washroom," she said, walking past the group of customers to the desk. An elderly, tough looking woman with grey hair followed in after her, talking in fast Italian.

Abby stopped them before they went to the back room. "I came to ask about the help wanted sign," she said. The little elderly woman looked her up and down, huffed, then walked away, mumbling to herself.

The other Italian lady smiled at Abby. "Great, you can start today."

* * *

A refreshing breeze drifted off the dark water, cooling Abby's sun burnt skin. She'd forgotten to put sunblock on before starting her work at the campground. The sky was dark now and the Skaha beach was deserted. All the festival events were happening on the Okanagan beach this time, so everyone was there tonight, which suited Abby just fine.

She'd worked all afternoon with the Italian ladies, who were also the owners of the campground. This was their busiest time of year, with another festival now in full swing, so they were grateful for the extra help. They agreed to let Abby stay at one of the sites for free while she worked there. It was a small campsite up on a hill, which didn't even have a spot for a vehicle to park, so no one had taken it yet.

After work, Abby had set up her small tent under a tall bush, tucked away out of the hot sun.

She hadn't heard from Jade all day nor seen him. But the campground was so over capacity at the moment, it wasn't a surprise she hadn't run into him.

The place looked like a survival camp after a tsunami. Sites that normally held one tent now had five or six set up in a circle all on the same site. The large garbage bins at the back of the campground were overflowing and the washrooms were a mess.

But it kept Abby busy cleaning, which helped her cope with the stress of being around so many people all in one place. She could just focus on her tasks and not talk to anyone. The Italian family didn't talk much while they worked, which was nice. Abby couldn't understand most of what the elderly Italian lady said anyway.

Now that the busyness of the day was over and she was alone, Abby couldn't help but worry about Jade. Why hadn't he contacted her? Was everything all right? She took off her sandals and let her feet sink into the sand. She was exhausted, but in a good way, and looking forward to lying down in her tent later.

Pulling out her cell phone, she checked it again. There were no new messages. Jade had sent a text earlier that he was on his way, but that was twenty minutes ago. Another breeze blew off the Skaha Lake and Abby closed her eyes. She breathed in the scents of the water, trying to settle her nerves. She had an uneasy feeling about Jade's silence. Was he avoiding her? Was there something he didn't want to tell her?

Abby opened her eyes and looked out across the water at the lavish homes nestled in the hills overlooking the lake. Their twinkling lights reflected off the water. What would it be like to live here, where there were festivals almost every weekend? Living here with Jade would be a dream come true.

As though materializing from her thoughts, Jade came walking across the sand. He waved when he saw her, looking as handsome as ever in a striped t-shirt and shorts. His serious expression made him look older. He usually smiled when he saw her but now he wasn't smiling. Maybe his reunion with his parents had gone worse than expected. She wondered what he'd told them about her, *if* he'd told them about her.

"You look beautiful," Jade said when he reached her. "How did you get such a nice tan in just one day?"

"That's what a hard day's labour under the sun will do to a person, I guess," Abby said, wrapping her arms around his neck and pulling him close. He slipped his arms around her waist, returning the hug. His firm body was so inviting, she wanted to jump up and wrap her legs around him, but thought better of it. They remained hugging for a moment, not saying anything.

"I got a job at the campground today," Abby finally said.

"Which campground?" Jade pulled back to look at her.

"Ours!"

"Really?" He smiled and took her hands in his. Suddenly she remembered where his hands had been last night, on her breasts. Her body flushed with heat. Was that really just last night? It seemed like only a dream now.

"I missed you," Abby said.

Jade didn't respond. Instead, he let go of her hands and walked to the water.

"My parents want me to go back to Vancouver early," he said, his back turned to her.

Abby's chest tightened. She'd been right, they were taking him away. Jade picked up a wayward rock on the sand and threw it into the moonlit waters.

"You should probably go back," Abby said, swallowing hard.

"I want to stay here, with you."

Abby remained silent. She wasn't going to persuade him to stay when he had more important things going on with his family, more urgent things. She wouldn't follow him to Vancouver either. Not yet. She'd wait until things weren't so complicated in his life.

Jade found another rock and hurled it at the lake. "What difference does six more months make anyway, in a damn hospital bed?" he mumbled to himself. At least that's what Abby thought she heard. Her stomach clenched. *Six months?* Did his mom only have six months left to live? But that was better than nothing... wasn't it? No, it was still too short a time to say goodbye to a loved one. No time could be long enough for that.

Tears stung Abby's eyes as she watched Jade's shoulders slump. He didn't look at her, he just looked down at the water.

"Jade!" a flustered female voice called out from the dark. They both turned. A young girl ran towards them on the sand, her long black hair flying behind her.

As she approached, Abby could see she had lovely brown eyes and a waif-like figure covered by a light summer dress which highlighted her perfect tan.

Jade frowned. "Hey."

"Hi! I'm so glad I found you," the girl said, catching her breath. She completely ignored Abby. "We've been looking all over. We're having a going away bonfire for you."

In the distance, down the beach, the flickering of a campfire caught Abby's eye. Jade looked in the same direction. "Do you want to go?" He asked.

The thought of joining a lively bonfire with a group of rowdy teenagers made Abby's stomach tighten. She wouldn't fit in nor enjoy herself.

"No." Abby put on her best smile for Jade. "I'm going to set up my tent stuff. I had a long day. You go on ahead."

"I'll come help you then," Jade said, putting a hand on her waist.

The dark haired girl's expression clouded for a second. Then she regained her composure. "You can come too if you want," she said to Abby.

"It's okay, I need to sleep." Abby turned to Jade. "Why don't you go and just come find me after the party?"

He hesitated for a moment. "Are you sure?"

Abby nodded.

"Okay, I'll see you after then." He gave her a quick kiss on the lips. The other girl looked shocked but recovered quickly, smiling at Jade as they walked off together. He glanced back at Abby, his silhouette too dark for her to make out his expression. She waved and smiled, but her heart sank as he disappeared into the night.

CHAPTER THIRTY-SEVEN

ABBY LAY IN HER TENT listening to the sounds of campers partying around her. It reminded her of all the times when she'd hid under the dessert table during her mom's dinner parties. She felt the same way now, alone yet surrounded by people.

It was too hot in the tent for her sleeping bag, so she lay on top of it, wearing only a light t-shirt and panties. Her fleece pajama bottoms were too warm and she was secretly hoping Jade would be pleased to find her in her panties when he arrived.

A wind rustled her tent and she turned onto her back, looking up at the branch shadows dancing on the tent walls. The longer she waited for Jade to return from his bonfire party, the more difficult it was to stay positive that he'd come. She didn't want to fall asleep but her eyelids were heavy and her body tired from the long day of work.

She rubbed her eyes. She had to stay awake. If Jade was leaving soon she wanted to spend as much time with him as possible, even if she was tired.

A heaviness settled onto her heart. How had she fallen in love with someone that wasn't available to her? He was too young. In a few years maybe, but right now it wasn't going to work. She'd been avoiding the obvious but now it couldn't be ignored any longer. She'd be turning thirty soon. Even though she looked younger she was still not going to fit in with his friends. Maybe just loving someone wasn't always enough. Was their age difference too much?

Tears streamed down Abby's face. She had to keep positive or the hurt would overtake her. Jade loved her and in a few years they could be together and maybe even get married.

Finally, at two-thirty in the morning Abby stopped hoping he would show up and fell asleep.

* * *

The sound of the tent zipper opening woke Abby from her sleep. Jade's hands glided up her bare legs before she even opened her eyes. She was laying on her stomach and he slid his fingers over the thin fabric of her panties, brushing over her bottom, then beneath her t-shirt.

Abby sighed at his touch. It *did* feel like drinking water when you're thirsty.

She turned onto her back and Jade's fingers moved to her tummy, then over her breasts. Abby looked up at him and smiled. He'd come after all, despite how late it was.

There was enough light coming from the lamp of a nearby campsite for her to see the sad expression on his face.

She sat up, reaching out to him. "Jade?" she said. "What's wrong?"

He kept his gaze down.

"If you need to go back home…" Abby said, but she couldn't finish her sentence. Her heart pounded painfully in her chest. Jade sat down beside her but remained silent.

"Your mom needs you right now," Abby continued, wanting to make his choice a little easier. She could only imagine how torn he must feel. "We'll see each other again later, even if it isn't for a long time. I'll wait for you."

Jade's eyes swam with emotion as he cupped her face in his hands.

"Abby, it isn't my mom that..." he held his breath for a moment. "Never mind," he said, tears filling his eyes. "You're right. We'll see each other again, I promise." His smile broke for a moment then returned. He gave her a heartwarming smile which ended way too soon. "I'm scared," he said softly. "What if there's nothing... after death?" His words trailed off into a quiet whisper.

"Of course there is," Abby said, with more conviction than she felt. She didn't know what she believed at that moment. All she knew was what Jade needed to hear. She touched his face, moving his hair away from his forehead. His eyes were full of tears.

He turned away. "Sorry," he said, his voice rough with emotion. He lay down onto his side. Abby didn't know what to do, what to say, to make things better. She reached out to put her hand on his shoulder then stopped. Would he rather not be touched when crying? Her chest hurt too much to cry. She couldn't do anything but hurt inside.

Jade turned onto his back with a heavy sigh, his face covered with both his arms. "I can't stop being scared," he continued, between short breaths. "Everyone looks at me like they're scared too, even though they believe in heaven and all that, but I don't see that in their eyes when they look at me. I only see…" he stopped talking.

Abby hugged her knees tight. "When I'm scared," she said, "I focus on something else. Or I sing." The lump in her throat made it hard to speak, but she began to sing anyway. She sang a song her dad used to sing to her at night when she was a little girl, when she was too scared to go back to school the next day. Her anxieties were always at their worst in the evenings.

As her song came to a close Jade's breathing slowed and he seemed to relax. Abby started the song again, repeating it until his hands slowly slid away from his face and he fell asleep. She let her voice trail off then lay down beside him.

CHAPTER THIRTY-EIGHT

AT SOME POINT IN THE early light of dawn, Abby fell asleep. She woke to the heat in her tent a few hours later and Jade was no longer there.

She checked her phone for the time.

10:30 am.

In half an hour she had to be dressed and ready to do the first washroom cleaning of the day. There wasn't time to get breakfast. Her phone had many text messages from Clarissa and missed calls from her mom. Maybe after the morning work shift she would look through all the messages and reply. None of them were from Jade so she wasn't in the mood to read them.

At the moment her head hurt and her heart felt heavy. She looked over to the empty spot where Jade had been only a few hours ago.

No, she couldn't start thinking about him now. It would do no good to stay here and be sad. It was only her second day of work and she didn't want to be late. She dressed with some difficulty in the small tent, then walked to the office to get a water bottle and pick up the work truck.

Martina was at the front desk. She was the feisty elderly lady's daughter. Martina's teenaged daughter, Gratia, also worked at the campground. Three generations all working together.

"Abby, so nice to see you. You're not leaving are you?"

"No, why?"

"I saw your boyfriend leave with his parents."

"Oh he's not my boyfriend."

Martina shrugged. "Then your late night friend."

Abby blushed. Martina must have seen Jade coming in and out of her tent. "Well, he is my boyfriend," she said, not wanting it to seem as though she had casual visitors at night to her tent.

"He checked out this morning," Martina said.

Abby frowned. "Oh, they checked out?"

"Si, yes. And I got this package half an hour after he left." Martina bent down to get something from behind the counter. She handed an Express Post package to Abby. "It has his name on it," she said, "and yours too."

Abby took the package and looked at the receiving address.

Abby Blosym c/o Jade Furlan

It was strange to realize she'd never known Jade's last name until now. And c/o meant 'care of' didn't it? Abby Blosym, in the care of Jade Furlan.

"Are you okay?" Martina asked, watching Abby.

"Yes," she smiled, "I'm fine."

Martina handed her the work truck keys, then Abby left the office, with the package in hand.

* * *

The day's work was a welcomed distraction. But by the time Abby was done with the washrooms and garbages she was starving. She walked to a nearby convenience store that was also a small diner which offered an all-day breakfast. Pulling out her cell phone, she finally looked at all her messages, while waiting for her food.

There were a lot of silly texts from her mom but she didn't reply to any of those questions. She simply wrote 'I'm fine, don't worry about me'. Guilt didn't plague her anymore the way it used to, so the short reply seemed enough.

There were a few messages from Clarissa asking how things were going. Abby did feel guilty for not replying to her yet. She took some time to type out a long text about Jade leaving and her staying here to work at the campground until the end of summer. She couldn't abandon the Italian family at their busiest time, and she actually enjoyed the work, which was surprising.

Feeling better for having dealt with her messages, Abby ate her late breakfast quickly, then headed back to the campground. She was eager to look at the package that had come in the mail.

Back at the campsite her tent was out of the hot sun, in the shade of the bush around it. She crawled inside, leaving the front entrance open for fresh air.

The package was on her pillow where she'd dropped it off before doing her morning work shift. She picked it up and opened it, emptying the contents onto her sleeping bag; two books and a beige drawstring bag. One of the books was a workbook, with lined pages, to write in. The other was a guide book. Abby leafed through it.

The images were drawn very realistically and made her feel awkward looking at them. But curiosity got the best of her and soon she wasn't as squeamish. The process looked a lot more complicated than she thought it would be. There was so much she didn't know about her own body, or a guy's.

Noticing the products mentioned in the book, Abby picked up the drawstring pouch and pulled out the sealed plastic bag inside. Her stomach clenched when she saw the large size of the smooth tipped object. It looked like a white plastic test tube, but larger. How would something so big ever fit inside of her?

Taking it out of the plastic bag she noticed there were smaller ones tucked inside the largest one, all fitting together like Russian dolls. The smallest one was no thicker than her pinkie finger. *This one's not that bad*, she thought.

The tent was getting too hot inside so Abby grabbed the workbook and sat outside to look at it. The sooner she worked through these questions and the program, the better. Even if she didn't end up having sex before she turned thirty, she just wanted to know that she *could* have sex. She'd do this for herself, to be free of her fear once and for all.

Abby spent the days in the same way; breakfast, cleaning, work on the Vaginismus self-help book, cleaning again and supper at the beach concession. She wanted to get through the entire Vaginismus program before her birthday at the end of the month. It was supposed to take much longer, but it was going really well and she'd been successful with the first few dilators once she learned how to do the muscle relaxation techniques.

Each evening, after a long hot day at the campground, the Italian family relaxed in folding chairs at the front of the campground entrance by the large gate. They watched the cars that came and went until

11 PM, when the campground closed for the night.

Abby decided to join them one night, not wanting to go back to her tent which still reminded her of her last evening with Jade. A few weeks had passed but she still missed him as though he'd just left.

"Iced tea?" Martina asked when she saw Abby approach. Nonna, the small elderly lady who was Martina's mother and only spoke Italian, stood watching the vehicles coming up the drive. She looked into each window to see if they were guests or just visitors.

Abby sat down at one of the chairs. "Sure," she said to Martina, who was already pouring her a glass of iced tea. "Does your mother ever stop working and relax?"

Just then Nonna ran up to a vehicle that was pulling into the driveway. "No visitors!" she said, waving her arms. Only the campground guests that were returning for the night were allowed past the gates at this hour.

"She loves keeping busy," Martina laughed.

"Where's Gratia?" Abby asked, taking a sip of her iced tea.

"Watching television." Martina looked at her. "How are you doing?"

"Me?" Abby took a big gulp of her iced tea. She knew what Martina was asking. She wanted to know if everything was all right with Jade.

"I'm okay," Abby shrugged. She was far from okay. The desperate feeling inside of her, of missing Jade, never eased.

"Are you sad because you came here to be with him and he left?"

"No," Abby said. "Well, I'm sad he left. But he had to go and I'll see him some time soon."

"But you came all this way from Alberta. You're not angry?"

"No, I'm not mad. And I didn't just come for him. I had to get away from my parents." Abby finished her glass of iced tea and set it down on the ground beside her chair. "And I had to come and help you guys out, right?"

Martina laughed. "Then I'm glad you came here for us."

"Me too," Abby smiled.

"There aren't many jobs here once the summer is over. Everybody leaves."

Abby nodded. "I figured as much."

"Will you move to Vancouver with your boy-friend?"

"No. I can't be a burden on him and I wouldn't survive out there on my own."

"Si, yes. I would never live out there. This is the best place in the world to live."

They sat in silence for a while, watching vehicles come and go. Martina knew the faces of each person that was staying at the campground and those who weren't supposed to be there at night.

Nonna disappeared, probably to take care of something else. Did that lady ever sleep?

Abby stayed until the gates were closed, then made her way back to her tent.

* * *

The final week of Abby's job at the campground went by fast. On the last day she woke to an overcast sky.

When she stepped out of her tent all the campsites were empty. The campground looked like a wasteland.

She looked up at the cloudy sky. Last night she'd successfully gotten through the Vaginismus program, except for the part about trying sex with a real guy. She wasn't blocked off or any of those things she'd worried about all these years. Jade was right, she just had to find a solution. Once she practiced the muscle relaxation techniques and retrained her reflexes so her muscles would stop closing up, it became easier to use the dilators and she was finally able to use the largest one.

But she didn't feel as happy about fixing her problem as she thought she would. The idea of losing her virginity as the solution to getting started on the next phase of life seemed silly now, without Jade.

Abby thought of Clarissa and smiled. She couldn't wait to tell her. Then she thought of Jade. If he hadn't encouraged her she'd still consider herself defective. Her embarrassing 'secret' which had haunted her all her life was now gone.

She could have dealt with it years ago. But, in a way, she was glad she hadn't. She wouldn't have wanted to lose her virginity to any of the other guys she'd briefly dated, or to Ben. Abby shivered. She'd almost married him. It would have been for all the wrong reasons.

She stood alone, overlooking the campground. She'd miss this place and she missed Jade so much. He hadn't messaged her, not once, and hadn't called either.

The work truck came around the corner, its tires crunching over the gravel and kicking up a cloud of dust. Abby waved to Martina and ran up to the window when the truck came to a stop.

"How are you feeling today Abby?" Martina asked.

"Good," Abby coughed as the dust settled. "I don't think I did half as much work as your mother did last night though." She shook her head. "She's amazing."

"Yes she is! You did a good job too. So you'll come and work for us again next summer?"

Abby nodded. "I'd love to. But we'll see."

"What are your plans for today? You can stay at this site as long as you need. Your paycheck is at the office."

"I'm going to…" Abby thought for a moment, realizing suddenly that it was her birthday today. How could that have slipped her mind? But it had been so busy with the cleanup and all. "I guess I'll go out for dinner tonight to celebrate my birthday."

What would she do for her birthday all alone? She'd done the same thing every year since she was seven, a family dinner at the country club. It was strange to be doing something else this year, by herself.

"Oh, how nice!" Martina said. "Will your boyfriend come to visit?"

"No." Suddenly Abby burst into tears.

"Oh, no…" Martina got out of the truck and ran over to Abby, pulling her into a hug. "I'm sorry. I say silly things sometimes."

"No, it's not you," Abby said, sniffling.

"I have the perfect thing for you today." Martina patted her on the back. "You will come with us to my cousin's wedding party. There will be the best food and dancing in town."

Abby shook her head. "I don't really feel like dancing."

"And we will celebrate your birthday, too. There is wine and maybe more money on your paycheck than you are expecting."

Abby wiped at her tears. "You don't need to do that…"

"It is already done." Martina put her arm around Abby's shoulders. "Come in the truck. We are going to get ready for the party. My daughter has a perfect dress for you to wear."

CHAPTER THIRTY-NINE

THE SKY WAS ABLAZE with the fading sunset, the perfect backdrop to the outdoor wedding. Little twinkling lights hung around the edge of a large tent canopy above the dance floor. The many flowers decorating the pillars and tables filled the air with a sweet scent.

Abby sat at a table near the back. She was pleasantly full from the six course meal at the reception earlier and now the food was making her too tired to dance. Not that she was in much of a dancing mood. The wedding reception was a nice distraction though. Everyone had made her feel like one of the family.

The Italian band on the stage, next to the dance floor, was playing a lively song with their guitars, singing words Abby didn't understand. But she loved the sound of their language. She tapped her feet along to the beat and smiled. Cousins, aunts, uncles, moms and dads were all dancing like nothing else in the world mattered. Abby envied them, wishing she could feel so care-free.

A cool breeze blew over her and she shivered. Dark clouds were making their way towards the outdoor party and the air smelled like rain.

"You're the only one not dancing," a male voice said, bringing her attention back to the table. A forty-something Italian man sat down in a chair next to her and smiled.

"Oh, I'm not a very good dancer," Abby said, looking away.

"Why do you look so sad?" the man asked. He spoke loudly, like most of the other male guests that were Italian. "Come." He took her hand and got up, pulling her to the dance floor.

He walked her right to the center of the stage, then finally let go of her hand. Abby hugged her arms around herself, feeling claustrophobic being surrounded by all the dancing people.

The fast song changed to a slower one and the frenzy died down as guests coupled off and began to slow dance.

"My name is Tony," the man said, offering his hand to her. Abby smiled shyly but didn't take his hand. She didn't feel like being touched. The man reminded her a little of Ben.

"Do you mind if I have this dance?" someone else said from behind her. She turned and let out a small gasp. Jade stood there, looking striking in a black suit and purple tie.

"Wow," he said, looking her up and down. "You look even more beautiful than I remembered."

Abby could only stand there, unable to speak.

Tony stepped back and nodded to them. "It looks like you have found a dancing partner now," he said, nudging Abby's arm with his elbow. He left to join a group of guys standing by the dance floor, talking loudly.

"Was that guy hitting on you?" Jade asked. He was smiling yet there was a hint of jealousy in his voice.

"How did you..." Abby couldn't think properly. She was so happy to see him that her hands trembled. "You came back!"

"Happy birthday," Jade said, reaching up to touch her cheek. Then his voice became quieter. "They were about to start treatments today and then my notification went off on my phone that it was your birthday and I had to come back for your birthday first."

"How did you know I'd be here?"

"I called the campground and asked if you were still working there. Martina gave me the address to this place." Jade smiled.

"So then you're just back for one night?" Abby swallowed hard, blinking back tears as Jade pulled her into his arms for a slow dance. His suit jacket buttons pushed gently against the thin fabric of her evening gown.

"I'm going back to Vancouver tomorrow," he said softly. "Then I won't be coming back again."

"Why aren't you coming back? What's going on? How is your mom?"

Jade's fingers clenched the back of her dress, forming into fists. "You have to promise me something."

Abby waited.

"Promise me," his breath staggered a moment. "Promise me that you won't come looking for me."

"What? Why would you say that?"

"Just promise," Jade said sharply, grabbing her by the shoulders. Abby stopped breathing for a moment. He had an angry expression on his face, but his eyes were filled with tears. What could be so terrible that he couldn't tell her? She'd told him every embarrassing thing about herself.

"Why can't you tell me?" she said, her heart squeezing in her chest.

Jade shook his head. He let his hands drop from her shoulders and looked down. "Please don't ask me to tell you."

"Is this about your mom?"

"No, it's not about her. If it was just about her I wouldn't leave you. I'd stay with you forever." Jade's tears escaped and ran down his cheeks.

"Okay," Abby said quickly. She tilted his head up and wiped away his tears. "If that's what you want. I won't ask. And I won't follow you."

"If I get through this, I'll come find you, okay?"

"Okay."

"I promise."

"Okay." Abby nodded.

"And then we'll be together and have a big slobbery dog and get matching tattoos."

Abby smiled, holding back tears of her own.

"And we'll go to Disneyland and Hawaii and I'll take you to a rock concert."

"What about your bucket list?"

"My bucket list only has one thing on it now. Being with you." Jade pulled her into his arms.

"But we still have tonight, right?" Abby said, each word cutting at her throat.

"Yes." Jade pulled back to look at her. "Is one last night together better than…than none?" he asked, trying to look her in the eyes, but she turned away.

"Yes." Abby nodded.

"Are you sure? Is it selfish of me?"

"No." Abby looked at him then and smiled. "I'm glad you came back for my birthday."

"I don't want to hurt you." The pained look on Jade's face tugged at Abby's heart.

"Don't be sad," she said. "Remember when you said what would make you happy was to pretend everything is fine and for us to be together as long as we can? Well, let's make tonight ours."

Jade nodded. He was here with her on her birthday, and that's what mattered. She wanted to capture this moment. She never wanted it to end.

The song changed to a faster beat and the dance floor filled with energetic dancers again. Abby had almost forgotten where they were. Jade took her hands in his. "Ready to dance?" he said with a smile.

"Yes!" Abby replied. She was ready. Tonight she wasn't going to be self-conscious and reserved. She had one night to be with Jade and to let herself be free.

He swung her in a circle on the dance floor and her hair flew around her. She lifted up her long evening dress and kicked her feet along to the music. A circle formed around them, cheering them on as Abby's dress spun.

Jade lifted her up by the waist, into the air, and Abby laughed. When he lowered her back down, he took her hand and spun her around again. The onlookers joined in on the dancing and soon the dance floor was alive with shouts of joy.

They danced on and on, spinning and laughing and being silly. Jade tired out first, pulling Abby aside to a nearby table.

"I think I need a drink of water," he said, his cheeks flushed.

"I've only seen wine to drink," Abby said over the music. Jade nodded and went to one of the dessert tables to pour them some wine. He returned with two full glasses, handing Abby one.

"I've never drank before, remember?" she said, taking the delicate glass from Jade's hand.

"Neither have I," he winked at her, then took a thirsty gulp. His expression went sour.

Abby laughed. "Is it that bad?"

Jade shrugged and tried again.

Abby tried a sip too. She expected sour but got an unexpected bitter taste. Her nose scrunched up and Jade laughed at her reaction. She tried another sip but her tongue kept curling in displeasure. The smell was nice enough, and it warmed her insides.

She give it another shot, taking a big gulp this time. Her eyes shut tight at the burning in her throat. Jade finished off his glass so Abby did too.

A loud clap of thunder cut through the sounds of laughter and music, and it began to rain.

Abby grabbed Jade's hand and ran for the cover of the dance floor canopy. They got there just in time before the rain started to pour down in sheets.

"Oh, no. The wedding!" Abby said. Yet, to her surprise everyone started clapping and cheering. "Why are they cheering?" she asked Jade.

"Rain on a wedding day means good luck and life-long happiness for the couple," Jade said. He squeezed her hand. "I'm half Italian." He pulled her close. "I want to be alone with you," he said close to her ear.

"How about we go to my place?" she whispered.

"Okay." Jade kissed her and excitement shot through her veins at the thought of all the kisses that were to come.

CHAPTER FORTY

RAINDROPS PLOPPED IN THE MANY puddles a few feet in front of Abby's tent. Jade sat with her at the entrance, and they watched the rain together. The large bush surrounding the tent kept most of the rain off of them and the air smelled of fresh dug up dirt and lake water.

Abby lay her head onto Jade's shoulder, savouring the moment. He still wore his formal clothes from the party, the dress shirt unbuttoned now at the top and the tie long forgotten.

Abby still had Gratia's dress on. It was all wet and clung to her body. She'd caught Jade glancing down at the front of the dress more than a few times.

"This reminds me of that first time we got caught in the rainstorm together," he said, wrapping his arm around her shoulders.

"If my feet didn't hurt so much from these high heels I'd go with you to the beach," Abby said. She smiled at the memory of jumping in the waves together, on a night just like this. It seemed so long ago. "I'm kind of unsteady on my feet right now though."

"I think it's the wine," Jade winked at her. He ran his fingers through her hair at the back of her neck, pulling her in for a kiss. "Your dress is so sexy," he said against her lips.

His hand moved down to the front of her dress as he kissed her, then he cupped her breast, his thumb running over her nipple which hardened through the thin fabric.

Abby deepened the kiss, pushing up against him. Jade didn't waste any more time. He pulled her inside the tent, closed the front zipper and stripped off his shirt. Abby smiled and set her hands onto his warm chest.

Jade placed his hands over hers. "All I think about is you" he said. "Your hair, your smile, your eyes, your body..." He leaned in to kiss her, smelling of wine and a warm scented cologne. "Abby?"

"Yes?"

"I want to…" His hand gripped hers tighter. "Do you want to—?"

Abby pushed him down onto the sleeping bag and climbed on top of him, pulling her dress up to her waist so she could straddle him.

Jade smiled as he looked up at her. "I wish you could see how beautiful you look right now," he said, his hands on her hips.

Abby slipped one strap of her dress off her shoulder, then the other.

"I wish you could see how happy you look right now," she said to him. Jade's smile brightened.

Abby peeled the wet fabric away from her breasts and Jade's eyes moved down to her nipples. She felt his reaction beneath her and he suddenly sat up. His warm chest pushed against her breasts.

"Abby…" he held her tight and she wrapped her arms around his neck. She could tell he wanted to say something so she waited. Instead he kissed her neck and she sighed, leaning her head back. He slowly tugged her dress up over her breasts, then over her head to remove it. Her hands got caught above her head.

"Just a minute," Jade chuckled, trying to untangle her. Then he stopped, laying her down onto the cool sleeping bag with her arms still caught in the dress. He held her arms above her head with one hand. With his other hand he caressed her body, from her neck to her knees then back up again. His fingers skimmed over the front of her panties. Abby bit her lip, trying not to squirm.

She closed her eyes, listening to the rain patter against the tent walls as Jade touched her everywhere. He let go of her hands and his lips began to trace the path of his fingers as he kissed her neck, then made his way down to her breasts.

He avoided her nipple, teasing her. Abby turned to the side, moving her breast towards his lips but he continued on his way down, kissing her tummy then the skin near her hip bone.

Abby giggled. "It tickles."

"Sorry." Jade sat up, his face flushed.

"No, I love it." Abby looked down and tensed when she saw his bulging pants. He seemed to notice where she was looking and removed his belt, setting it off to the side. Then he lay onto his back, hands behind his head, as though offering himself for her exploration.

Abby touched her warm cheeks and looked away. "I'm a little nervous," she said.

"Me too." Jade reached his hand out to her. "Come here. We can just lay here together."

Abby scooted over to him, but remained sitting. "This is so different than how I imagined," she said.

"What do you mean?" Jade asked. She ran her hands over his firm stomach muscles.

"The idea of being sexual with someone always seemed so scary and weird. But with you, it's... fun." She smiled. "Because I feel safe with you."

Jade closed his eyes and Abby lay down next to him, snuggling up. She rested her head onto his chest and made circles on his belly with her finger, working up her nerve to touch him lower down. Jade's breathing became deeper. Was he falling asleep?

Abby slipped her hand below the front of his pants. He sucked in a breath, pulling his stomach muscles in to give her hand more room. The top of her fingers brushed the tip of his warm skin beneath his pants. She stopped. She wasn't sure what she'd expected but warm and smooth hadn't been it.

Jade took her hand and gently guided it down further. She wrapped her fingers around him and slid her hand down then back up again. Jade moaned so she did it again. After the third time he clasped her wrist to stop her.

"Wait," he said.

He undid his pants and pulled them off.

"Here, let me help." Abby tugged at his boxers but then the sight of him made her shy. She turned away. Yet there was also a twinge of excitement stirring inside of her.

Jade tilted her chin up and turned her towards him. "Are you... able to try? Did you get that package in the mail?"

Abby nodded.

He touched her cheek then ran his thumb slowly over her bottom lip, his gaze distant.

"What is it? Is something wrong?" Abby asked.

He smile faded. "I don't want to do the wrong thing," he whispered. He looked into her eyes, his expression serious. "I can't marry you right now and take care of you—"

"Jade, I want to make love to you, more than anything I've ever wanted."

He threw her onto the sleeping bag and kissed her with urgency. His sudden passion burned through her from head to toe. Each time the tips of their tongues touched Abby felt a throbbing between her legs.

She dug her nails into Jade's back, pulling him down onto her. He resisted a moment, just long enough to reach down and slide her panties from under her bottom to remove them. He tossed the panties aside and lowered himself onto her. Their bellies touched and his chest pressed gently onto her breasts. Abby wanted to hold him like this forever, with no clothes coming between them.

Jade repositioned himself and she felt pressure near the spot where she was moist. Her body tensed.

"Wait," she said, taking his hand. She closed her eyes. *I can do this.* "Okay." She opened her eyes again and looked at Jade.

"Okay," he said, smiling.

"I have to squeeze and relax my muscles like I practiced," she said. He nodded and smoothed back her hair with his hand.

"No rush," he said. "If you don't want to—"

"I do," Abby said. She squeezed his hand at the same time as she squeezed the muscles inside of her, then relaxed, and repeated. "I'm scared," she whispered.

"Look at me," Jade said softly, turning her face towards him. "You'll do just fine." He gave her a gentle kiss on the lips.

Abby nodded. She squeezed his hand again then relaxed it, returning to the rhythm.

"When I relax—" she started to say.

"I get it," Jade said against her lips.

She turned her face to the side again, holding back a grin. "I have to focus, quit distracting me." Starting again, she squeezed for three seconds then relaxed for three seconds and repeated.

Jade kissed her slowly, patiently waiting. She felt him slip a ring onto her finger but was too distracted by her squeezing and relaxing to think about what he was doing.

Then she was ready. Her hand relaxed. Before she could tell Jade he suddenly thrust into her and she cried out in surprise. Pain shot through her, so intense that the insides of her ears burned like they were on fire. Then, just as fast as the pain had come, it left. Her body broke out in a cold sweat. She let go of Jade's hand.

She'd done it.

Before she could start to cry, pleasure flowed into every part of her. Jade was inside of her, on top of her, wrapped around her, one with her. They were as close as any two people could ever get.

"Are you okay?" he asked, his voice a little shaky. He didn't move as he waited for her reply.

"Yes." Abby whispered.

Jade relaxed, pulling back a little.

"No..." Abby dug her nails into the small of his back to pull him close again. "Stay close."

Jade pushed against her in response and she gasped, this time out of pleasure. He continued the movement and her legs slipped up and around his waist. She arched her back and got up onto her elbows, moving with Jade as he pushed against her, the pleasure building quickly.

Jade's lips found her breasts. The cool wet of his tongue shot heat straight between her legs. She throbbed with desire. His lips closed around her nipple and she grabbed the back of his head, pushing more of her breast into his mouth.

"Oh...Jade!" she cried out, at the thrill of climax. Jade moaned releasing her breast and capturing her mouth with his. He thrust one last time as they both reached the height of their pleasure. Abby's body shivered with delight, then she dropped back onto the sleeping bag.

"I love you," Jade whispered.

I love you too, Abby thought, but she couldn't seem to speak. Her eyes flooded with tears. Jade held her a moment before they separated. Then he collapsed onto the foam mattress beside her.

"Are you okay?" he asked.

"Yes," Abby said, finding her voice. She was still tingling, her body blissfully satiated.

Jade pulled her into his arms and covered them up with the unzipped sleeping bag that had gotten bunched off to the side during their lovemaking. Abby settled into his embrace, the most perfect moment of her entire life. She closed her eyes wanting nothing more than to remain in his arms forever.

CHAPTER FORTY-ONE

ABBY TURNED THE PLATINUM BAND round and round her ring finger, trying to remember how it got there. But whenever she thought back to her evening with Jade a heaviness settled onto her heart, one that she couldn't bear.

She got up, wiping away the tears that kept coming. A rush of cold air over her bare chest reminded her she was naked. She pulled the sleeping bag close and covered her face with her hands, then started to cry again. The pain was unbearable. But there was no point in thinking about Jade now. He was gone and she needed to get dressed and get some food.

Scrambling through her pile of clothes, Abby dug out her flannel pajamas to wear on the way to the washroom for her shower. There weren't a lot of clean clothes left. She'd need to do another load of laundry at the Laundromat soon. But then again it didn't really matter, she was going back to Alberta anyway. A note beside her pillow caught her eye. She picked it up with a shaky hand.

Happy Birthday Abby

I love you

Now you are free xoxox

She set the note back down onto the pillow and turned away from it. Grabbing her bag, she slipped on a pair of flip flops and headed out of the tent.

The girls' washroom was deserted; no blow driers humming loudly or curling irons on the sink counter.

There was no chatter or laughter of sisters doing their make-up side by side in front of the mirrors. Only silence.

Each sound Abby made echoed through the empty space. She shuffled her flip flopped feet to one of the showers and banged open the stall door. Everyone had left and returned to their lives, except for her.

Reaching up to deposit coins into the coin slot, Abby stopped and looked at the ring that Jade had put on her ring finger. It fit a little loose. She would continue to wear it there, even though people would surely ask about it. But first she'd need to get it sized.

Abby put the coins in the slot and the sound of the water starting filled the silence. She removed her ring, not wanting it to slip off her finger and roll away when she soaped her hands. She set it on top of the coin box, then noticed the engravings inside.

Jade and Abby ><><

She stared at it a moment. What was the diamond-like symbol? Was it just a trademark of the jeweler or did it have some other meaning?

The hum of the water pipes reminded her that the time for her hot water was running out. She set the temperature to as hot as she could handle and climbed in.

The heat warmed her skin, but she shivered nevertheless. The only thing that would ever take away the chill inside of her was being in Jade's arms again. She wanted to cry, but couldn't. What had she done? Why had she given her heart to someone that was too young for her and she couldn't be with?

"Ouch!" Abby doubled over in pain, a sudden cramp in her lower belly catching her by surprise. She straightened, smoothing back her hair from her face. Were things on the inside of her supposed to feel different after having sex for the first time? Had anything changed inside her body? She had no idea what to expect.

She smiled then. Despite everything, she *was* happy, deep down. How could she not be? She'd lost her virginity, finally, and to someone amazing. Someone she was in love with.

Abby closed her eyes and saw Jade's smiling face. Did he feel different today, wherever he was at this moment? She held back a sob.

They should have had breakfast together this morning, talking in hushed tones about their night, while sitting in a booth at some breakfast diner. She'd wanted to wake up naked together and make love again in the tent, before going out to eat. But Jade had left in the middle of the night. Why didn't he wake her to say goodbye? Her eyes burned, but there were no tears left to cry.

She couldn't blame him for leaving without a goodbye, just the note. It would have been too hard on her to hear it from him.

Abby finished her shower quickly and got dressed. She went to the sinks to brush her hair and looked up at the foggy mirror. It blurred her reflection so she wiped the moisture away with her hand. Her eyes looked back at her in the mirror, bright and alive, her cheeks rosy pink and her lips like two red rose petals.

I wish you could see how beautiful you look right now. Jade's words came back to her.

And then she saw it. She saw how beautiful she actually was. Was this what Jade saw last night, when he'd looked up at her when she was straddling him and said those very words, as though looking at the most precious thing in the world?

She'd always thought of herself as plain and unattractive, but that's not what she saw now in the mirror. She did feel different after spending the night with Jade, very different. She liked the reflection in the mirror for the first time in her life, and not because she'd finally made love to someone, but because she'd found love. Abby smiled at the mirror. *Now you're free*, Jade had written. He was right, she was free.

Even with all the emotional pain and everything else, the car crash, the tears and living in a tent, she'd had no panic attacks, not one. How strange. The campground job was hard work and yet she'd done just fine. The campground had been crowded with people but she'd stayed and didn't get claustrophobic.

Visions of her last night with Jade came to mind every time she closed her eyes, but she didn't stop them. She saw the silver watch he wore on his wrist, the only thing he'd been wearing as he kissed her lips, then her neck, then her breasts. She remembered the careful way he touched her everywhere, the passion in his eyes when he looked at her body, the love in his eyes when he looked at her.

Jade loved her. She wasn't any less worthy of being loved, even if she couldn't have sex. He would have still loved her either way. But he couldn't be with her.

Abby's smile faded. She knew he was the one who was sick. When had she realized? When they'd written their bucket lists? But she'd denied it to the very end. He hadn't wanted to talk to her about it. He didn't want her to look at him differently. He didn't want her to know.

It was easier to pretend, to ignore how easily he got tired out sometimes, the fear in his eyes, the distant looks, the unspoken desperation that she not find out he was sick.

Abby pushed her palm against her chest and let out a small cry. That's why he didn't want her to follow him to Vancouver. She took in a deep breath and stood up straight. It was a bad idea to think about all of this right now. The grief would just consume her and she'd fall apart.

She had to focus on other things, like cleaning up her campsite and depositing her paycheck so she could buy a bus ticket back to Alberta and return with her head hung low. She couldn't stay here. Everything reminded her of Jade: the beach, the town, even the moisture in the air. She could smell him close by and hear him and see him at every turn.

The empty prairies would be a good place to mourn, until she knew whether or not Jade would get better and if they had a chance to be together again someday.

Until then, Penticton would remain her happiest place, with all her perfect memories.

Later on that afternoon, on the bus ride back to Alberta, Abby drew.

She drew Jade with her, swimming in the lake, the large waves rising up during the thunderstorm. She drew them looking down over the Fun Zone amusement park from a rope bridge high up in the air, Jade's arms wrapped around her so she'd feel safe. She drew their fateful meeting at the beach vendor tent when she'd been hoping to run into him one last time before returning home.

Then she drew Jade waiting for her outside of her hotel room, their first kiss at her house, and Jade drawing ravens on her chest by candlelight.

Lastly she drew them wrapped up in each other's arms, suspended in air while kissing, her hair surrounding them.

She stopped only when her hand cramped and she couldn't hold the pencil anymore. She hadn't drawn with such passion since high school. Closing her sketch book she looked out the window at the Rocky Mountains, oblivious to their beauty or to anything else around her. All she could see was the absence of Jade beside her.

CHAPTER FORTY-TWO

"**A**RE YOU READY FOR BREAKFAST?" Jade asked Abby. They were in her tent but it was bigger, with white bed sheets and sunlight streaming in through the sheer canopy surrounding them.

Abby lay naked on her back. She took Jade's warm hand and set it on her breast. He bent over her and kissed her neck, her shoulder, then her chest.

Abby closed her eyes, waiting. When Jade's kisses stopped she opened her eyes again.

"Jade?" She sat up, looking around. But he wasn't there. The tent became small and dark. A newspaper clipping crinkled beneath her hand and she picked it up. It was an obituary with Jade's picture.

"No!" she screamed, waking up from her dream. The walls of the tent were replaced by the walls of Abby's childhood bedroom. Her body was drenched in sweat. Jade hadn't called or texted in weeks. She didn't know if he was sick or okay.

The sound of his voice still hung in the air, as though he'd just been in the room seconds ago. Abby could smell his warm scent and she cried, her sobs uncontainable as she pulled the blankets over her to try and drown them out.

* * *

"I suppose everyone needs a good rebellion at some point in their lives," Abby's mom said, passing the mashed potatoes. "I just wish you wouldn't have waited so long to do it. You're thirty now and at your age it reflects poorly on us."

Abby ignored the comment. Her dad looked up from his plate but didn't say anything.

"Can you pass the pepper?" Abby asked. The painful dreams she was having each night since she'd moved back in with her parents, two weeks ago now, always left her feeling weak and hungry all day. She'd even agreed to work as a receptionist at one of her mother's offices in town. She'd wanted to get her own job, her own way, but had no ambition or energy lately. Worrying about Jade, missing him, consumed every part of her.

The office job was fine for now. The sooner she started working the sooner she'd be out of this house and in a place of her own, although finding a decent apartment was proving very difficult so far.

"Abby, you're eating too much, leave some for the rest of us," her mom said. "I've already gone grocery shopping twice this week."

Abby stopped mid-bite of her bun. "I'm sorry for eating your food, Mom," she said coldly, setting down the bun.

"That's not what I meant and you know it." Her mother began cutting the asparagus on her plate into tiny pieces.

"You don't even do the grocery shopping. Sofia does," Abby said.

"I just mean," her mother continued, "that you don't want to gain too much weight, at least not until after you're married. And the clothes you've been wearing lately, the baggy pants—"

Abby stood up. "You never stick up for me!" she yelled at her dad. He'd been sitting there quietly and now stopped drinking his juice.

"I'm leaving." She pushed out her chair and stormed off.

"Wait," her dad followed after her, but she didn't stop. She kept going until she was at the front door, with her coat and purse in hand.

"I'm going to stay at a hotel for a few days until I find a place of my own. I've got some money," she said to her dad.

"Here…" He pulled his wallet out from his back pocket.

"No, dad…"

"I want you to use whatever you need. You don't owe me. You're my daughter."

Abby didn't reply.

"You can deduct from your paycheck whatever you use, once you start working, if you'd like," her dad continued. He handed her a charge card. "I always wanted to make lots of money so I could buy you things, but you never ask for anything."

"I used to ask, but mom never let me buy anything." Abby shook her head. "Never mind it doesn't matter." She took the charge card. "You can stay with her Dad, but I can't take it anymore. I'm leaving. I really don't think you should have to stand for it either."

Abby put on her shoes and left, wanting to get away quickly, before she started crying again. She wasn't sure how she'd made it even a day living back at her parents' place, but the past two weeks were plenty enough. Her mother's comments were too toxic, especially with the pain of all that had happened lately. Abby didn't need any of it. If she could live in a tent for two weeks, she could live anywhere.

It didn't take long to find a place to live when you weren't picky. Abby put a down payment on a rundown apartment in a building that had a pub on the bottom floor. She'd avoided even walking in front of places like this in the past, but with the way she was feeling lately, she didn't even care if she got mugged.

The apartment smelled like mold, the walls were yellow from cigarette smoke, the maroon carpet was stained in more than one place, there was a hole in the drywall, a crack in the window and the heater made noises. Not to mention the club music at night, on Thursdays, Fridays and Saturdays. The bass rattled the dishes in the sink. But it kept her company on those lonely nights.

Clarissa was away on a trip with Matt, again. They were visiting his grandparents in Ontario this time, and wedding shops along the way. When she returned and heard that Abby had a place of her own, she came over right away.

"Your mom is paying you a fair wage isn't she?" she asked, stepping into the apartment with her high heels.

"Yes." Abby took her jacket. "But I don't start work in the office until Monday. My mom had to give Sharon two weeks' notice."

"Sharon the secretary? I thought there was an opening for General Manager." Clarissa lifted a foot to remove her fancy high heels, then, seeming to think better of it, she left them on and walked over to the couch to have a seat.

"You get used to it," Abby said with a grin on her face. "After a couple of weeks it doesn't seem that bad anymore. I didn't want the manager job. Receptionist is fine. My mom offered Sharon the promotion to General Manager but she didn't want it either. Who would, with my mom being the boss."

Abby took a seat beside Clarissa and shifted uncomfortably on the couch. "You're probably right about those Lactaid pills. I'm so bloated and my pants never seem to fit anymore. I should take three when I have ice cream, not two."

"How much ice cream did you eat?"

"A tub full."

"A tub full?" Clarissa's eyes went wide.

"Just one of those small containers." Abby showed the size with her hands. "Or maybe medium sized. Actually, now that I think of it I'm pretty sure it was lactose free ice cream. It must have been that cheese pizza then."

"How much of that did you eat?"

"Just one."

"One slice? Two Lactaid pills should have been enough for that."

"No, one whole pizza."

"An entire small pizza?" Clarissa glanced down at Abby's tummy.

"Medium pizza actually, they were on sale. Two for one."

"Abby..." Clarissa patted Abby's stomach lightly. In the position Abby was sitting, it did look really bloated. "Why are you eating so much anyway? You never eat, you're always so picky about food."

Abby shrugged. She knew the answer. She was eating non-stop because she was depressed. But she didn't want to worry Clarissa.

"What happened with Jade?" Clarissa asked, a concerned look on her face. "Did you two—?"

"Tell me about your engagement," Abby cut her off. "Did you set a date for the wedding yet?"

"You're changing the subject."

"I don't want to talk about Jade. It's too hard." Abby's eyes flooded with tears, which came all too easily these days. She couldn't stop them, she couldn't control her crying, at the grocery store, at the thrift store, at the library. She stood up, feeling shaky and tired with the sudden wave of grief that came upon her. "Can you come back some other time? I'm just really tired."

"It's only seven." Clarissa stood up too.

"I ate too much and it makes me tired."

Clarissa put her arms around Abby in a hug. "I'm worried about you," she said.

Abby didn't hug her back. It would only make her cry more if she did. Instead, she let her arms hang loosely at her sides and said nothing.

"Do you want to see someone?" Clarissa asked, pulling back from the hug. "About your sadness?"

"No!" Abby snapped.

Clarissa stepped back, a hurt expression on her face.

"Sorry," Abby said. She walked over to the small kitchenette to get a glass of water. "I'll be fine tomorrow. My stomach is bothering me. Maybe I'll take another Lactaid pill." She took out a pill and popped it into her mouth. "So did you find a nice dress while you were in Ontario?"

Clarissa's eyes lit up. She was about to reply but then stopped. "It's not important," she said with a frown.

"Don't worry about me." Abby grabbed a cup of water and drank to wash down the pill. "I don't want my moodiness to rain on your parade. Tell me all about the pretty dresses."

"Are you sure it's just moodiness?" Clarissa said.

A sudden wave of dizziness caught Abby by surprise and she gasped, reaching for the edge of the kitchen counter and dropping the glass in her hand. It shattered on the linoleum floor.

Clarissa jumped in surprise. "Are you okay?" she said, rushing over.

"Don't!" Abby put her hand out to stop her. "You'll step on the glass."

"Is that...?" Clarissa grabbed Abby's outstretched hand and turned it over.

"Why are you wearing a ring on your wedding finger?"

"Because I can't get it off, okay?" Abby pulled her hand away. The broken glass on the floor made her want to cry. She didn't have many glasses, just the four she'd bought at the second hand store, now three. They weren't expensive but she couldn't hold back the tears.

"Clarissa, please just go." Her voice trembled. Clarissa's presence was upsetting the routine of Abby's little world. She hadn't been feeling good for the past few days and now it was all finally catching up with her. "I'll call you when I'm not feeling so... emotional, okay?"

Abby didn't look up to see Clarissa's reaction. "Please?" she said, feeling nauseous.

Clarissa walked to the door and opened it. As soon as it clicked shut Abby began to sob. She pulled at the ring on her finger again but it wouldn't come off. Her finger was swollen, probably from all the salty food she'd been eating lately and her body retaining water.

She didn't care if she was gaining weight or retaining water. She'd eat and gain a thousand pounds if it would help her feel better. She also didn't care if she lived in a rundown apartment with all the other rundown people of the world, those who'd had the smile slapped right off their faces by the cruel realities of life, just like she'd had.

She took out her dust pan and broom and began to sweep up the shattered glass on the floor. She didn't want to wear Jade's ring anymore. She didn't want to miss him so much. Maybe Clarissa was right. Maybe she should go see someone for her sadness.

CHAPTER FORTY-THREE

"IS IT HOT IN HERE?" Abby asked Jessica, a cleaning lady who worked for her mom's business. They were the only two in the office that afternoon.

"No, not too hot," Jessica said, looking at the schedule posted on the bulletin board. She was in her early thirties and had a Mexican accent. Her long black hair was pulled back into a ponytail, as it was every day.

"You have a flu maybe?" She glanced over at Abby.

"I hope not." Abby rubbed her eyes and leaned back in her seat. She'd been staring at the computer screen for a while, going over the month's cleaning supplies order list.

"You look sick," Jessica gave her a worried look.

"Maybe I do have a virus." Abby sighed, pushing her chair back from the computer desk. A sudden heat rushed through her, from head to toe, and her stomach heaved. She jumped up from her chair but there wasn't enough time to make it to the washroom. She grabbed the nearest garbage can and threw up into it.

"You should go home," Jessica said. "The answering machine is working just fine. You don't need to be here if you are sick."

"I already missed half a day yesterday because I was nauseous." Abby gathered the garbage bag together and removed it from the basket. Jessica took it from her to deposit out back.

"Thanks." Abby sat back down. Her first week on the job and she was already taking sick days. But she was glad that Jessica was in the office just then. At least the cleaning staff wouldn't think she was taking time off for no reason, or just because she was the owner's daughter.

"It's Friday," Jessica said, returning with a replacement bag for the garbage. "You can leave early."

Abby nodded. She was tired and ready to go home. "I didn't eat much today," she said. "It just upsets my stomach when I think of food."

"Mrs. Blosym…"

"It's Miss."

"Oh, you are not married?"

"No."

"Do you have a boyfriend?"

Abby frowned. "No, why?"

"Then I am sure it is just a virus. It will go away." Jessica patted her on the arm. "I give my kids the pink Bismol, for stomach problems."

"I didn't know you were married with kids."

"I'm not married now. I came to Canada with my children." Jessica glanced down at Abby's ring finger. "You are a Miss but you have a ring on the married finger?"

Abby shook her head, covering her hand. "I'm not married." She was getting tired of saying that to everyone who asked. Maybe she'd just start telling people that she *was* married, and leave it at that.

"You came to Canada all on your own, with two small kids? You're so strong Jessica."

"You are strong too," Jessica said. She gave Abby's arm a squeeze then went to get her purse from one of the waiting chairs. "Here." She handed Abby a small container of Pepto Bismol chewable tablets. "It's for the children but it will help you, too."

"Thank you." Abby took two of the pills from the bottle. "I'm sure I'll be better by Monday."

Jessica nodded. "You are not like your mother," she said.

"Thank you. That's a really nice thing for you to say."

"Here is my phone number." Jessica pulled off a sticky note from a pad on Abby's desk and wrote her number down. "If you are more sick or need to talk, you call me." She handed over the note.

"Thanks," Abby said, blinking back tears. She was definitely ready to go home.

CHAPTER FORTY-FOUR

ABBY DREAMED OF JADE again. She ran her hands over his firm stomach muscles. He played with her hair, his gentle movements arousing her desire to make love.

She climbed on top of him and kissed him. His body was warm beneath hers. He ran his hand down her back and onto her bottom. Her desire grew even more and she reached down to undo his pants.

"Abby, don't!" Jade pushed her off of him and then she was falling, down through the ground and into a dark void.

Abby woke with a cry and threw up over the side of the bed. Her stomach clenched and soon the next wave of nausea came.

She ran to the toilet and threw up again. Her body shook. *Oh God please make it stop.*

When there was no food left to throw up she continued heaving anyway.

Why hadn't she gone to a walk-in clinic yesterday after work? But she didn't have a fever and had been so tired.

Now she was too sick to go anywhere. Surely she'd die right here, in front of her toilet, of grief and sickness.

When the heaving finally stopped, she wanted to cry, but didn't have the energy to. There was no one she could call. Her mother didn't really care about her, not in the ways that mattered.

Her dad didn't *do* anything. Plus, he couldn't drive here at 2 AM without her mother knowing about it, which would only make things worse. Clarissa was happily engaged and soon to be married. Then the baby would come and she'd forget all about Abby and take prenatal classes with other pregnant moms and make new friends.

And Jade... Was he sick and still in the hospital? Was he going to die? Would she really never see him again?

The reality of it hit so hard that Abby couldn't be strong anymore. She didn't want to think of him being sick, the way she was feeling now, or maybe worse. She didn't want him to be scared the way he'd been on the night he cried in her tent. She would take his place and be sick for the rest of her life if it would make him better.

A half hour later the worst had passed and Abby slowly made her way to the living room couch. She got into a sitting position that helped her feel the least nauseous and reached for her cell phone. Then she wrote a message to Jade.

I know u're the one who is sick and not ur mom. I miss u so much. Can I come see u? ...please?

Her finger hovered over the send button. She looked at the words until they swam in front of her eyes. Finally, she deleted the message. Then, noticing Jessica's name in her contacts list, she wrote a new message.

Hi Jessica this is Abby. I'm really sick and sad and I don't want to be alone.

She didn't expect a reply to come so soon, but it came a minute later, asking for her address. Abby sent the information and stayed on the couch until Jessica showed up fifteen minutes later.

"This is for you," Jessica said, handing her a white paper pharmacy bag.

"Thanks." Abby took it and returned to the couch while Jessica removed her shoes. She couldn't stay standing too long, without feeling sick again.

"How are you?" Jessica asked, joining Abby on the couch.

"I'm okay if I just sit still." Abby tucked her legs up. "Where are your kids? You really didn't have to come over at this time."

"They are fine. They are with my mother. She lives with us in the house. They will be okay. I am more worried about you." Jessica took the paper bag from Abby and emptied the contents onto the couch. A bottle of Tums Antacid and a pregnancy test kit came tumbling out.

Abby froze. Her mind took a moment to register the idea. Pregnant? But she couldn't be. She'd only had sex one time. For her mother it took almost five years to finally become pregnant with Abby. She never imagined one time could...

"Maybe you can try this test?" Jessica said, rubbing Abby's back.

Abby couldn't think straight. She couldn't deal with all the emotions coming at her all at once. Excitement at the possibilities, fear of being this sick for nine whole months, and also joy, worry, anticipation...

Jade's bucket list had "have a baby" on it, and so did hers.

Abby's hands shook as she picked up the pregnancy test. She got up and took it with her to the washroom. This would be the longest three minute wait of her life.

CHAPTER FORTY-FIVE

BEING SICK FOR A PURPOSE, a grand purpose, was much better than being sick just to suffer. Every nauseous feeling Abby felt, every instance of heartburn or fit of vomiting in the middle of the night, every tired moment; they were all evidence of a little baby Jade growing inside of her. She didn't care how sick she was. She just wanted this baby be born healthy.

After visiting the doctor and getting medication for the nausea, which was safe to take during pregnancy, Abby was feeling a bit better. She also got folic acid pills. The large prenatal vitamins made her too nauseous, so for now she was just on the folic acid, which would help the baby.

Monday morning she walked into her office, a little slower than usual, but doing much better. She was looking through next month's work schedule when Jessica came in to return her cleaning supplies for the day.

"Still working too hard?" Jessica asked, coming to her desk.

"Or hardly working," Abby smiled. "How are you?"

"Better than you are, I know." Jessica returned the smile.

"I'm just looking over next month's schedule," Abby said, glancing back at the calendar. "Do you have any requests for time off over the holidays?"

"No, just Christmas day. The rest I will work, for extra pay of course." Jessica winked. She walked over to Abby's desk and pulled out a tiny pair of blue knitted baby slippers from behind her back. "My mother knit a present for the baby."

"Oh, it's beautiful!" Abby got up from her chair, bumping her tummy on the desk's pullout keyboard tray. The small bit of belly growth was still going unnoticed by others, so far, but not by Abby.

"And," Jessica pulled out another pair of slippers from behind her back, pink this time. "Two colours, for a girl or boy."

"Thank you." Abby took the slippers and gave her a hug.

"What will you name the baby girl? And if it is a boy, what will you name the boy?"

"Jade, whether it's a boy or a girl," Abby said.

"Oh, I like that name."

"It's—"

"Abby?" Her mother's sharp voice startled them both.

"Mom!" A chill ran down Abby's spine.

Her mother was standing at the door with a shocked expression on her face.

CHAPTER FORTY-SIX

"AND I HAVE TO OVERHEAR this from the *cleaning staff?*" Abby's mother said the last two words between clenched teeth. She'd dismissed Jessica from the office and was now in full self-righteous mode, upset at not being the first one to know about Abby's pregnancy.

"I'm not even in my second trimester yet," Abby replied calmly. She was leaning back against the receptionist desk, her nausea returning. "I wanted to wait to tell people. The doctor said a lot of first time pregnancies can get miscarried in the first trimester."

"Oh," her mother visibly relaxed. "Well," she flipped her hair back over her shoulders, looking down at Abby. "With your size right now I only assumed..." she indicated towards Abby's belly, which was sticking out a bit as she leaned back against the desk for support. "Well I could only assume that you were farther along." She dug through her purse and took out her check book. "How much money do these things cost?"

"What things?" Abby asked, straightening up.

"Oh, you know," her mom waved her hand in the air. "Taking care of unwanted pregnancies."

Abby's hands clutched the edge of the desk in a death grip. Had she heard her mother right? "What makes you think this pregnancy is unwanted?" she asked.

"Don't be difficult Abby." Her mother took out a pen and set the check book down on the desk to sign it. "Fine. I'll just sign the check and let you fill in the amount once you find out. But only the amount for that, nothing more." She handed Abby the check.

"Thanks." Abby snatched it from her hand and ripped it up.

"Abby!"

"Don't ever talk to me again," she said in a low voice. She stood in front of her mother's stunned face for a moment, forcing her to make eye contact, then stormed out of the office.

Even her stomach knew better than to mess with her at that moment. She took the stairs two at a time and drove straight to the cell phone store to ask them how she can block all phone calls and incoming text messages from her mother. She wasn't going to listen to any more of what her mother had to say. Not for a long time to come, if ever again.

CHAPTER FORTY-SEVEN

This WILL LAST YOU ALL WEEK!" Jessica said, stirring the large pot on the stove. She was making Mexican Beef Stew in Abby's apartment.

"You didn't have to come all the way here to make it for me," Abby said from her position on the couch. She was enjoying the couch more and more each day. Her appetite was finally returning and her belly was showing it.

"Of course I have to come here!" Jessica called over the commotion of her two young children. Gabriella and Javier were chasing each other with dinosaur toys. "Do you think I want to mess up my own kitchen at home?"

Abby laughed, watching the kids run past her. Jessica's kids were the cutest. Gabriella was four, with long dark hair like her mother's and beautiful big brown eyes. Javier was six, with the same colour hair and eyes, but he was smaller than Gabriella, even though he was two years older than her. She was a healthy weight, while her older brother was as skinny as a rail, which gave her the advantage in sibling fights.

"Mama! Gabriella took my dinosaur!" Javier whined. He crossed his arms in front of his small body and pouted. Gabriella had two dinosaurs in her hand now and a big grin on her face.

"Gabriella!" Jessica called from the stove in a stern voice, but the little girl only giggled and ran away.

Abby put her hand over her belly, wondering what little Jade would be like. She was in her second trimester now and becoming more hopeful.

The last two months felt like she'd been holding her breath the entire time, crossing her fingers that nothing would happen to make her lose her unborn child. She wouldn't be able to handle it if something happened to this baby, who she could now feel moving around inside of her.

The thought of there being an actual child in her belly was so surreal. But the ultrasound had confirmed it. He or she was growing at a regular rate and didn't have any problems. Abby had paid to have an ultrasound done, just to help her stop worrying about there being problems with the baby.

The smell of the beef stew wafted into the living room area and made Abby's stomach growl. She was grateful to have some homemade cooking now that she was eating regularly again. Her small apartment felt like a real home, with the kids and Jessica taking over the space. They were unfazed by the stained carpet and yellow walls and had settled right in with no trouble at all.

"Here you are." Jessica came over to the couch with a pile of envelopes in her hand. "This was in the kitchen." She handed Abby the pile and took a seat beside her. "The stew will cook now until it is ready."

Abby sighed and took the envelopes from Jessica. She'd been avoiding looking at her mail, worried that there would be more bills. She wasn't going back to work for her mom, and had to look for a job again. But getting hired while pregnant wasn't easy. She'd taken her dad's offer of financial help until she could find a job again.

"I hope there aren't more bills," Abby said, sorting through the pile.

"Soon it will be Christmas and they are taking extra workers at the mall, just for the seasonal work," Jessica said, putting up her feet on the coffee table. Abby smiled, glad that Jessica felt at home here. She never wanted to have a house that was so nice that kids couldn't mess it up or spill things.

"That's a great idea, I'll see what positions are available..." Abby stopped. A large brown envelope said *Comic Arts Undiscovered Talent Competition*. It was addressed to her. She opened it and took out the papers. At the top was a letter.

Congratulations!

> *Your comic book is this year's 'Comic Arts Undiscovered Talent Competition' winner!*
>
> *For the grand prize, we are excited to offer you a publishing contract for your comic book. Find enclosed with this letter all the guidelines needed to finalize this process. The production editor also had a few notes, which*

are included. The paperwork is a preliminary draft of your comic book publishing contract.

Please look this over during the next 14 days. Our office will contact you on Thursday Dec. 18 at five-o'clock.

Abby stared at the letter, speechless.

"Is everything okay?" Jessica asked, inching closer to her on the couch to look at the letter. "Is it bad news?"

"Mama…" little Javier whined.

"Not now Javier," Jessica said, "you watch the cartoon show on the TV." She waved him away, then rubbed Abby's back. "Is it a letter from the father?"

"No… well in a way, I guess it is." Abby swallowed hard, blinking back tears. She'd never entered her work into a competition. Jade must have sent in her comic booklet that she'd tossed at him when he was leaving to return to Penticton.

The memory gripped her heart. She could still see the heartbroken expression on his face, like it had just happened yesterday. He'd flinched, catching it just before it hit him in the face.

She tried to hold back the tears as the children watched the television. Jessica pulled her into a hug.

"I just want to see him," she mumbled into Jessica's shoulder.

"Then go. Where does he live?"

"In Vancouver, but I can't—"

"Oh, that is expensive. I'm sorry."

"And I don't know where he lives."

"You know his last name, no?"

"I…" Abby stopped crying for a moment. She'd seen Jade's name on the package he had sent to the campground in Penticton. It started with an F. She thought for a moment. "Furlan. Yes, I know it."

"Then you can find him."

Abby sat up, wiping away her tears. "You're right, Jessica. I'm going to Vancouver."

CHAPTER FORTY-EIGHT

ABBY'S FEET ACHED as she walked the final block to the church. The bus had dropped her off two blocks away, but fortunately the beginning of December wasn't too cold in Vancouver. It was, however, raining. The umbrella she'd bought at the airport kept her dry, but her sneakers were soaked through.

The air smelled of fresh grass and the overcast sky was a perfect backdrop to her mood. It had been a long drive to the airport, then the flight to Vancouver, and finally the bus ride here. She had no idea what to expect when she reached her destination.

She should have tried to contact Jade earlier, when she first found out she was pregnant. But he'd made her promise not to look for him. He said he'd contact her if he got through it all, and she knew he meant it. But he hadn't tried, so he was still not ready to see her.

She walked on, through the quaint neighbourhood, with its nicely cut lawns and clean driveways. This was the kind of place you'd feel good about settling down in, to start a family.

Abby was happy to finally see the church building's tall ceiling in the near distance. Her tummy had grown and her back hurt whenever she walked too far. But she was in no hurry to reach the church either. She hadn't figured out yet what to say to Jade's father, or if she should say anything about the baby at all before she saw Jade. First she had to find out where he was.

She reached the church sooner than she would have liked. Rubbing the small of her back with one hand, she stopped at the doors. A middle-aged man with a blonde mustache and black suit jacket came out, opening the door for her.

"Please come in, do you need any help?" he asked her.

"Oh, I'm sorry," Abby said, stepping inside. "I didn't realize there would be a church service today." She sighed. After being unsuccessful at reaching Jade on his cell phone or finding their home address, she decided to come to Mr. Furlan's church, which had an address online.

"We have a funeral today," the man said. Abby's breath caught.

"Whose funeral?" she asked, her voice barely above a whisper.

"The Pastor's son." The usher's voice sounded like it was coming from another room. Abby lost her balance. The front hall spun before her eyes. The usher caught her by the elbow, helping her stay upright.

"Come have a seat," he said, leading her to a nearby chair.

"No," Abby regained her composure, but her hands trembled. "I'm fine."

Freeing herself from the usher's grasp, she walked forward, her legs having a mind of their own. She didn't want to go in. She didn't want to be in this place. But she went ahead until she was in the main church area, near the back pews. A man was speaking at the podium, his voice amplified by the microphone in front of him.

Mixed in with his words was the sniffling and crying from the people in the pews. Abby wanted to turn and run, but she couldn't move.

"Jade was always a positive thinker," the man at the podium said. It was apparent by his looks that he was Jade's father. "He never rebelled, not even when he crashed his car this summer, it wasn't out of rebellion. He'd gone and found himself a girlfriend, I suppose…"

Mr. Furlan had deep bags under his eyes. He wore a dark suit and tie and his voice trembled slightly as he spoke. "He used all of his savings to buy a platinum ring in a small size." Mr. Furlan shrugged, a small grin on his face for a moment. There were a few sad laughs from the congregation.

"One thing," Mr. Furlan continued, "that Jade wanted more than anything, was to have a child of his own."

A hush fell over the room.

"When he turned eighteen, and was still doing fine, after so many years… he'd been doing just fine, all through high school, I thought… surely…" The Pastor's voice broke with emotion as he blinked back tears.

"Surely he would have time to have a family." He took a moment to regain his composure before continuing. "I'm sorry. I can't do this." He looked up. "With all these doubts, and anger at God. It isn't fair to you all. I am resigning from my position as Pastor of this church, as of today."

Everyone gasped. Abby was still standing at the back, the pain in her feet and back long forgotten. She stepped forward now and began to walk down the aisle. A few heads turned in her direction.

Heart pounding, she went to the front then stopped.

"Mr. Furlan?" she said. He looked at her with tired, red eyes. "You don't have to resign…" Abby unzipped her heavy jacket to show her growing belly.

EPILOGUE

TWO YEARS LATER....

LITTLE JADE STUMBLED on his small feet, racing for the shiny wrapping paper by the Christmas tree.

"Jade, honey, look at what grandma got for you," Abby's mom said, rolling the Easy Rider Truck over to him. Jade paid no attention as he took a seat in the pile of crinkly paper. He crumpled it in his hands and shoved a fistful into his mouth.

Abby and Charles got up at the same time to stop him from eating it. Charles got there first and pulled the paper out. He'd really taken to Jade. Despite the hair colour difference, everyone always thought he was the biological father.

Abby smiled as she watched Jade and Charles throw crumpled up balls of wrapping paper at each other.

"I don't see why Jade has to go to some silly church potluck while you're away," Abby's mom said. She got up off the floor and smoothed out her perfectly ironed skirt. "They see Jade every weekend."

"But you're getting him for the whole week mom," Abby said.

"And you're sure it's safe to fly to Los Angeles all by yourself?"

Abby's dad and Mr. Furlan walked into the living room from the kitchen, where they'd been discussing business.

"I'm at a comic convention," Abby said to her mom. "I'll be at my artist booth all day. I don't think anyone's going to attack me with thousands of people around."

"And there will be lots of Storm Troopers there if anything bad should happen," Charles said. Abby's mom huffed, knowing she was missing the joke.

Charles pulled more wrapping paper out of Jade's mouth. "I think he may be getting hungry."

Abby's mom picked him up. "I can go feed him."

"I don't mind," Mrs. Furlan said, also getting up. She'd been sitting on the couch quietly, as though deep in thought, but now reached for Jade. "You fed him the apple sauce earlier."

"Well, he likes it when I feed him." Abby's mom held Jade close, turning him away from Mrs. Furlan's reach.

"Shall we go try out those new cigars Charles brought back from Cuba?" Abby's dad said to Mr. Furlan.

"What would the congregation think if they heard you were smoking?" Mrs. Furlan said to her husband.

"I agree with Thelma," Abby's mom chimed in. "It would give the teenagers in your church an excuse to start smoking."

Abby rolled her eyes, exchanging glances with her dad. He smiled. They were used to this banter by now.

"Shall we?" Abby's dad said to the other two men, ushering them towards the back patio doors. Her mom was already in the kitchen with Jade and Abby was left in the living room with Mrs. Furlan.

"I can't believe I'm going to L.A.," Abby said, staring up at the Christmas tree.

"Jade would have been very proud to hear about it," Mrs. Furlan said. She gave Abby a sad smile. Abby could only imagine how hard the holidays were for Jade's parents now that he was gone.

"Little Jade looks just like his father did at this age," Mrs. Furlan said, dabbing at her eyes. She picked up her purse. "Before I forget, I brought you something." She pulled out a small teddy bear ornament with a name tag that said 'Jade' on it. "This was Jade's. We got it on his first Christmas." She handed Abby the ornament.

Abby took it with both hands. "Thank you," she said, blinking back tears.

"Maybe it can be little Jade's now." Mrs. Furlan said.

"I'll put it on the tree." Abby got up and hung the ornament on a branch. A loud squeal came from the kitchen.

"Themla! A little help here, if you don't mind," Abby's mom called.

Mrs. Furlan grinned. "Coming."

"I don't know how she raised me when I was a baby," Abby whispered. Seeing Oggy on the floor, she picked up the ragged Ogopogo stuffy and handed it to Mrs. Furlan. The toy had become Jade's favourite stuffed animal that he never went anywhere without.

"Jade will be looking for this."

"I'll take it to him," Mrs. Furlan said.

Abby watched her go and then she was alone, in a rare moment of silence. She went back to the tree to look at the ornament.

"Well," she whispered, "you were right Jade. My comic books are doing well." Abby smiled. "Your son is amazing. He looks just like you and he's got my mom wrapped around his tiny little finger. It's nice to see someone have control over her for once. Your mom adores him too."

Abby wiped at her tears. "Merry Christmas Jade," she said. After a moment, she turned to go to the kitchen to see what all the squealing was about. Just then Charles came in, holding a Nanaimo bar on a small plate.

"Sorry," he said, stopping when he saw the expression on Abby's face. "I didn't mean to interrupt. Do you need a moment alone?"

"I'm okay," Abby sniffled, taking a seat on the couch. Charles joined her and set the plate down on the coffee table. Abby smiled. He still remembered she loved Nanaimo bars, since their first meeting at her parents' anniversary party over three years ago.

She'd grown fond of him in the past year since he'd moved to Vancouver. He was helping her dad start his new company after Ben had taken the old one. Charles was a great manager and her father credited the success of his new venture to Charles' efforts.

Abby had moved to Vancouver to be closer to Jade's parents, who'd been desperate to be with their grandson. She also started her career as a graphic artist here. This city was better suited to the arts and entertainment world than the small one she'd grown up in.

Whenever Abby went to her dad's office to visit, Charles would make a point of talking to her and eventually she gave in to his charm and finally said yes to a coffee date. Clarissa's wedding had been easier with him at Abby's side. And he didn't seem to mind that most of their dates involved playing with a toddler.

Charles was now her manager too, with her comic series publications, and also a close friend.

"You look so serious," Charles said, studying her.

"Just thinking." Abby sighed.

"About Jade's father?"

"Yes."

"You still miss him a lot, huh?"

Abby didn't reply. She didn't want to cry, even if Charles had comforted her many times before, when she'd cried over missing Jade. Jade wouldn't want her to be sad on Christmas Eve.

"I know you've been anxious to get your ring back," Charles said, fiddling with a tiny box in his hands. Abby glanced at him curiously. Charles never fidgeted. He was always confident and sure of himself. He'd offered to get her ring cleaned and shined.

"I was going to hire a string quartet." He turned the box over and over in his hand. "And set up Christmas lights out on the back porch."

"Charles," Abby said. "It's cold and raining outside." She set her hands onto his, to stop him from playing with the box.

"But I just couldn't wait any longer," he continued. "This ring has been burning a hole in my pocket. I got it back over a week ago." He got down on the carpet in front of her and set the small box in her lap, opening it. Abby gasped.

"My ring..." Her platinum ring was fused with a new one, one with a sparkling diamond at the center.

"Abby Elizabeth Blosym," Charles said, his hazel eyes swimming with emotion. "Will you do me the honour of becoming my wife?" He took her hands in his. "I know I can never replace Jade..."

"I..." Abby's words caught in her throat. Charles had been so good to her and patient. She would never feel the way she'd felt about Jade towards anyone else and Charles knew that. He understood that. His first wife had died in a plane crash and he'd vowed to never replace her with another woman.

He was young when it happened, only twenty-five, and since then he hadn't dated or made love to a woman for over ten years. That is, until this year. Abby had reached out to him, selfishly taking affection from him, but also giving. They had a surprisingly normal and loving relationship despite the pain in their pasts.

"I don't think anyone should ever replace him," Charles continued. "I just want to take care of you, and little Jade, for the rest of your lives. I love you, Abby."

Abby threw her arms around his neck.

"And…" Charles returned her hug. "Maybe, if you are ready one day to have another baby, maybe little Jade can have a little brother or sister."

"Yes," Abby said, the tears flowing freely now. "I would love that."

Charles relaxed into her embrace and let out a sigh. "I wasn't entirely sure you'd say yes, you know."

Abby kissed him. "You've been so good to me, and Jade," she said. "And I love you, too."

Charles removed the ring from the box and slipped it onto her finger. "I think I was supposed to put this on while asking you."

"No," Abby smiled, "your proposal was perfect."

Holding her double band close to her heart, Abby closed her eyes and listened to the lively chatter of her mom and Jade's mom in the kitchen, with interruptions by Jade's squeals of delight. Her relationship with her mother had been hard to heal but little Jade had made it possible. There was no denying how much her parents loved him, their one and only grandson.

"Let's go help my mom with Jade," Abby said. Charles nodded and they got up together.

Abby's mom and Mrs. Furlan were wiping splotches of food off of their dresses when Abby and Charles walked into the kitchen. Jade giggled and threw more food onto the floor from his highchair.

"Oh good, you're here," Abby's mom said. "I don't suppose you know of a dry cleaning place open on Christmas Eve, do you?"

Abby and Charles laughed. Mrs. Furlan smiled at them, as though sensing their sudden change in relationship status. Abby was grateful for her kind heart, and to everyone at her house that night. She was glad they were all part of her life. Jade would be glad to know his son was making them all so happy.

Abby leaned over and kissed him on the forehead. Whenever she looked at her little boy she saw Jade, and that made her the happiest of all.

THE VIRGIN DIARIES PLAYLIST

AT THE PEACH FESTIVAL
Jade serenades Abby on a karaoke stage.
The inspiration for this scene and song:
"Kiss You" by One Direction

IN ABBY'S APARTMENT
Jade serenades Abby in her apartment with a song he
wrote for her. The inspiration for his lyrics from:
"Stuck in the Moment" by Justin Bieber

HOW JADE FEELS ABOUT ABBY
"When I See You Smile" by Bad English
"Tonight" by Ace Troubleshooter

HOW ABBY FEELS ABOUT JADE
"When I Look Into Your Eyes" by Firehouse
"More Than Words Can Say" by Alias

ABBY'S PAIN OF LOSING JADE
The chorus of the heart-breaking song:
"Tonight" by F.M. Static

THE VIRGIN DIARIES DISCUSSION QUESTIONS

1. Abby's controlling mother affects her decisions even as an adult. When do you believe Abby truly breaks away from her influence?

2. What do you think was the biggest factor in Abby's fear of sex? Was it physical or emotional or psychological?

3. Why do you think Jade didn't tell Abby he was sick?

4. What do you suppose the symbol is on the ring Jade puts on Abby's finger? (hint, it is not the infinity symbol)

5. Put yourself in Abby's shoes. Would you spend one last night, intimately, with someone you fell in love with, before they left and you never saw them again? Or would it make losing them even more painful?

6. Are there issues that you don't discuss with others because they seem embarrassing? Do you suppose others have similar issues but no one ever discusses it?

7. Have you ever told someone you trusted a difficult secret and then felt better afterward? Did it give you strength to face it or fix the problem?

8. When did you realize Abby was pregnant?

9. Do you know someone like Jessica? Do you have a friend like her or are you such a friend to someone else?

10. If you were Abby would you have let your mother back into your life after she was so uncaring about your pregnancy situation?

11. How would you have ended the book differently and why?

12. What do you think Abby's life would have been like had she married Ben?

ACKNOWLEDGEMENTS

This book would not exist without the kindness and support of:

my best friend (and editor) Amanda, my brilliant editor Kaleen and my original beta readers Shannon and Pam;

my husband David and daughter Jessica, who patiently tip-toed around the house whenever I was writing, and my mom who is always there for me;

my critique friends Emily, Amber, Kirstie, Ian and Ken, who've helped me become a better writer;

my workmates Robab and Shirin, who read my novel online and gave me advice, and Dustin who helped me through the formatting nightmare;

my awesome writer's group The River Bottom Writers;

the beautiful Svitlana for posing as the front cover model,

and of course thanks be to God for giving me everything I need to make my dreams come true;

and to all the readers, especially my wattpad readers, thank you all.

BIANCA ROWENA

The author of The Virgin Diaries, was born in Transylvania, Romania and raised in Southern Alberta, Canada, neighbour to the beautiful British Columbia, which served as the setting and vacation spot for The Virgin Diaries. She now lives with her husband and daughter in Alberta, Canada.

Visit her online at www.biancarowena.com

FOLLOW BIANCA ROWENA ON

ALSO AVAILABLE AS AN EBOOK

CPSIA information can be obtained
at www.ICGtesting.com
Printed in the USA
LVHW041122141121
703288LV00005B/655